Cedric the Bulge

Neal Wooten

ISBN 978-1-61225-431-9

Published by Mirror Publishing
Fort Payne, Alabama 35967
www.pagesofwonder.com

Printed in the USA

For Regina Grayson,
who introduced me to Cyrano de Bergerac

Even if a king defeats his enemy in battle, that still doesn't settle anything. There are other, less numerous armies of philosophers and scientists, and their contests determine the true triumph or defeat of nations.

One scholar is matched with another; one creative mind with another; and one judicious temperament with his counterpart. A victory won on that field counts for three won by force of arms.

- Cyrano de Bergerac

CHAPTER ONE

\

"Who is that?" the handsome young stranger asked, not sure if what he saw was real or a vision. "Seriously, who is that?"

Roger Sims glanced up. His interest was piqued so he looked around to see to whom the person was referring. Seeing no one else nearby, he walked out from behind the counter and over to the glass entrance door to look for himself. "Oh, that's Roxy Clifton. She's the head cheerleader at Frenchtown High."

Frenchtown was a small town in the southern part of Tennessee with a population of a little over 20,000 residents. In the center of the town square was an idyllic park with one huge oak tree, which was well over a hundred years old, and several wooden benches where old timers sat and fed the pigeons.

Businesses of all kinds lined the outer sides of the square-shaped road like clothing stores, two banks, antique stores, appliance repair shops, hardware stores, auto shops, the post office, city hall, the police station, a laundromat, and a few restaurants including the Frosty Freeze where Roger worked. Beyond the commercial area in every direction were the residential homes and about fifty churches. It was a peaceful semi-paradise almost right out of a Norman Rockwell painting.

Roger walked back to his position behind the register as the stranger continued to stare out the window like a puppy dog seeking a new home. The glass was even beginning to fog up in a small circle in front of his lips.

The guy couldn't move because Roxy, who had been standing beside a car and talking to friends, was staring back at him, and the link between them at that moment was as tangible and taut as a steel cable.

Roxy was physically stunning, five feet tall with natural curly blonde hair. Her jeans seemed to be painted on. In fact, everything about her was a work of art, Mother Nature being the Rembrandt. Finally, Roxy's friends coaxed her into the car and they drove away.

Only then did the strange young fellow turn away and walk to the counter. "What's her name again?"

"Roxy," Roger answered as he looked the guy over. He had never seen him before. The guy stood almost six feet tall, had neat sandy-brown hair, a chiseled face, which included a prominent dimple in his chin, and was built very well, slender but with well-defined everything. Veins protruded from his lean arms. His blue eyes almost looked like pools of Windex. He wore Levi jeans with a white Polo shirt. "Who are you?" Roger asked.

"Oh, I'm sorry," the guy said sticking out his hand. "I'm Chris Nevil. My family just moved here from Western Hills."

"Will you be going to school here?" Roger asked.

Chris nodded. "Yes, I will, and playing football I hope. I'll be a senior."

"I guess I'll see you in school then." Roger was also going to be a senior but not an athlete. He was a geek in every sense of the word, including very smart, and the editor of the school newspaper. He was small and weak with thinning blonde hair, much too thin for his young age. His family owned the Frosty Freeze, which served burgers, hot dogs, pizza, fries, ice cream, and all manners of good old Americana food. It had been the popular hangout for the students of French-town for generations. "Did you want to eat?"

"No," Chris said. "I was just wondering if you guys were hiring."

Roger smiled. "No, it's strictly a family business, just me, my mom and dad, and two sisters."

"So tell me about Roxy," Chris said. "Does she have a boyfriend?"

Roger shook his head. "She's very nice, but very picky."

That news boosted Chris's confidence. He was used to girls finding him attractive, which was a good thing since he was not a smooth operator at all. He usually became quite tongue-tied around females.

"Yeah," Roger continued. "She's very smart and only likes to date smart guys."

Chris stopped smiling. "Seriously?"

Roger nodded. "You might try the grocery store across the square or the feed-and-grain mill on the out-skirts of town."

"What? Oh, for a job? Yes, I will try those. Thanks. I guess I'll see you in school in a few days."

Roger waved as Chris walked out.

Chris's mind, however, was far from job-seeking at the moment. In fact, over the next three days, he could only concentrate on one thing. He went to the town square as much as he could, going in the stores and shops. Two more times he saw Roxy, both times again at a distance, and both times they stared at each other for several minutes. It made Chris's heart go pitter-patter, but thanks to what Roger had told him about her, it made the acid in his stomach activate the proverbial butterflies and he found himself becoming nauseated as each staring contest progressed.

Finally the first day of school came and Chris dressed up and drove his rusty 1967 Mustang and parked in the student parking lot. He garnered several stares as he walked into the building and found his way to the office.

"I'm Chris Nevil," he said to the woman behind the counter. "Today is my first day."

The woman picked up a manila folder from under the counter and held it up in the air as she continued with whatever paperwork she was doing. "Nice to meet you, Chris. I have your file right here. Principal Wilson wants to see you first."

"Am I in trouble?"

The woman did not look up. "He likes to meet all the new students. Have a seat right there." She pointed to two empty, metal folding chairs against the wall.

Chris sat and waited. A young girl, an office aide it appeared, couldn't divert her eyes from him. Chris smiled and nodded but her constant glare was beginning to make him uncomfortable.

"Nevil?"

Chris looked up to see the principal standing in the entrance to his office. "Come on in and close the door behind you."

The woman handed the principal the manila folder.

He did as instructed and walked into the small office. One small lamp barely illuminated the small space. The blinds on the windows allowed for very little sunlight to enter. A large window air conditioner was blasting away making a steady humming noise, cooling the small office to the point you could hang meat. Chris sat on the leather sofa when the principal nodded toward it.

The principal took his seat in a big leather swivel wingback. He was a very tall man, dressed to the nines, clean-shaven, with a slight gut. He silently and intently began reading over Chris's file.

Chris patiently waited. The leather upholstery made the room seem even colder and he had to concentrate to keep his teeth from chattering.

"Football!"

Chris looked up. "What, sir?"

"Says here you play football."

"Yes, sir."

"Are you any good?"

"Yes, sir."

"See that trophy there?" Principal Wilson motioned with his head again.

Chris looked at the three-feet-high trophy behind the glass of the tailored case. It was the only trophy in the case and appeared to have been custom made for that one trophy. Many other trophies and plaques from varying sports and organizations filled several long cases that adorned the hallway walls, but this one was revered among all others.

"Yes, sir," Chris answered.

"That's from 1954, our only state championship. Can you believe that?"

Chris recognized a rhetorical question and didn't answer.

"You're not going to answer?"

"Oh, sorry," Chris said. "No, it's hard to believe."

"I was part of that team," the principal said with a proud smile as he shifted his weight back in his chair.

"That's amazing, sir."

The principal leaned back forward and looked again at Chris's file. "Hard to believe you made the honor roll several years at your old school. I was pulling your leg. I was only six years old in 1954."

Chris chuckled at his own gullibility.

"But I do remember what it did for this town," the principal said. "I would love for the folks in this town to feel that again. You understand what I'm saying?"

Chris nodded.

"Okay." He handed the folder to Chris. "Go by and see Coach Edwards today and sign up for the team."

"Yes, sir." Chris took the folder back out to the woman.

She took the folder and pulled out a half-sheet of paper. "Here's your schedule." Turning to look the young girl who had been devouring Chris with her eyes earlier, she added, "And Gwen here will show you around to get you started."

The cute sophomore with flowing auburn hair and soft brown eyes took the paper and walked around the counter. She still couldn't stop staring at Chris, or grinning. "Come on; I'll show you where everything is."

"Thank you," Chris said and followed her out the door of the office.

As they walked, Gwen pointed out everything she could think of: lockers, water fountains, bathrooms, and even cracks in the ceiling. But mostly her focus stayed on the new student.

As for Chris, he continually scanned the faces in search of the one above all others he wanted to see.

"Hey, Chris."

Chris looked around and saw a familiar face. "Hey, Roger."

Roger took the schedule from Gwen. "Let's see here. Well, we don't have any classes together so I guess I'll see you at lunch." He pointed to the schedule. "We both have second lunch. And, I assume you will be coming to the pep rally tonight."

Chris looked confused as Roger disappeared into the crowd.

"You are coming, aren't you?" Gwen asked.

"I didn't know about until now, but I guess so."

Gwen's grin widened. "Here's your homeroom."

Chris smiled and entered as Gwen slowly walked away.

The day wore on as Chris went to all his classes but, unfortunately, he never saw Roxy. Third period was his Study Hall class and he was excused to go to his meeting with the football coach.

"Come on in, young fellow, and have a seat."

The coach's metal desk was up against the side wall, so Chris sat in the chair right beside him. The coach was a short stocky guy in his mid-thirties. He had large scarred arms and huge round shoulders, and a very thick neck, well, what was visible of it. It was almost as if his head sat right atop his shoulders.

"So you wanna play football?"

His voice was the deepest Chris had ever heard and he looked to Chris how an English bulldog might look as a human.

"Yes, sir."

The coach looked Chris over. "Good. I'm sure we can use you. I guess you've already heard that this could be the year we go all the way."

"I've heard that. I hope so."

Coach Edwards nodded. "What position did you play at your other school?"

"Wide receiver."

"We'll see," the coach said. "We have some great talent, a good quarterback and good runner, and the best lineman in the country. Have you met Cedric?"

Chris looked confused. He had not even heard the name until now.

"Well, you will." The coach stood giving Chris his cue. "You need to get a form signed by your parents and we'll get you your exercise gear."

Chris shook his hand and went back to Study Hall.

After the next class, which was basic math, lunch

time came and Chris followed the crowd to the cafeteria. He got in line, which ran alongside one wall, took a full plate from one of the lunchroom ladies, and paid at the cashier. There were no choices for food. Everyone ate the same thing.

He found a table that was empty and sat there. He stared at the food with little enthusiasm.

"Room for one more?"

Chris looked up and saw Roger and smiled. "Of course." As Roger took a seat across from him, he wasted no time. "I haven't seen Roxy all day."

Roger laughed as he started pulling his own lunch out of a brown bag: A hamburger and fries from his family's restaurant. Even cold it looked better than the school food. "You probably won't see her much. She takes all advanced classes. And she has first lunch. Hey, don't worry," he added seeing the disappointment in Chris's face. "She'll be at the pep rally tonight."

Chris nodded.

"Did you get on the football team?" Roger asked.

"Yeah. Why?"

"Well," Roger said, spinning around and pointing. "Those are their tables over there. You could go sit with them."

Chris shook his head. "I don't feel like one of them yet."

Roger understood. "Well come on by the Frosty Freeze at 1:00 on Saturday afternoon. All the players meet there, even the new ones. It's a tradition. And let's you and I get together in the next few days so I can get some information and write an intro about you in the school paper." He then leaned forward and whispered. "Roxy loves to read the school paper."

That brought a smile to Chris's face.

"In fact, I got to get back to the paper pretty soon." Roger began to eat a little faster.

Chris looked back at the two tables of athletic students eating and cutting up. He thought about going over and introducing himself, but decided against it. He knew they would all have a chance to meet him at the restaurant or at practice.

Then he saw him. There in the middle of one of the tables was the biggest student he had ever seen. He might have even been the biggest human he had ever seen. It seemed every student around him leaned toward him almost as if he was a planet and the gravitational pull was too much. He was facing in Chris's direction and Chris could make out the features of his face since he towered above the guys seated across from him. "Who is that?"

Roger didn't even have to turn around to know to whom Chris was referring. "Cedric."

Chris's eyes lit up. "The coach told me about him; said he was a great lineman."

"He is that," Roger said, "and a whole lot more."

"What do you mean?"

Roger smiled. "I mean he's also a genius, the smartest guy you will ever meet. He's a great writer, a math whiz, and a wonderful poet." Roger wadded up his bag. "I've got to go. See you this evening."

Chris waved then returned his attention to the giant football genius. *Poet?* he thought. *What kind of guy, especially a football player, writes poetry*? You would certainly never catch Chris writing poems, even if he could.

The rest of the day passed. When school was over, Chris drove home. After he finished his homework, he ate supper with his mom and dad.

"A pep rally tonight?" his mom asked.

Chris shrugged. "That's what everyone said."

"You're part of the team now, son," his dad said, "so you are expected to go."

Chris nodded. He wanted to go, mainly because he never saw Roxy all day at school but knew she would be at the pep rally tonight. He had practiced several opening lines for when they finally got a chance to speak, but wasn't happy with any of them. And he still got nervous just thinking about her.

After he helped his mom put away everything and helped her with the dishes, he dressed up again and drove back to the school.

"Hi, I'm Chris. What's your name?

"That's lame," Chris said to himself looking in the rearview mirror. "She probably knows by now I know her name.

"Hi. You're Roxy.

"Idiot. She knows her own name."

Chris swallowed hard and tried to think of a better line. The shadow-talking continued all the way to the school with nothing he believed would make a good first impression. He was a little late and most of the student body was gathered on the football field. He followed the lights and joined in. He looked all around and finally found the cheerleaders. And there she was.

Roxy and the other five cheerleaders were in uniform at midfield.

He squeezed his way through other students until he had a clear view and watched her for several minutes. She was a true vision. Chris's hands began to sweat.

The squad performed organized cheers and stood around talking amongst themselves and other students in between.

Chris waited patiently hoping Roxy would find him.

Finally she scanned the crowd and her focus locked with Chris. Their eyes did the same dance as each time before.

Chris was frozen. He wanted to walk over but couldn't move. He tried desperately to recall the best line he had come up with before remembering he never came up with a single decent opening line. So they stared and stared. Finally he swallowed hard and took a step in her direction.

"Hey, Chris."

He broke the stare, stopped, and turned around. "Oh, hey, Gwen. How are you tonight?"

"Great... now. I'm glad you came."

Chris nodded.

"I hear you made the football team."

"Yeah, I guess so," Chris said. Of course he didn't know what the word "made" meant since he just asked the coach who looked him over and said "okay."

"That's wonderful," Gwen said. "I know you'll do great."

Chris smiled. As much as he wanted to be concentrating his focus somewhere else, he didn't want to appear rude.

"But I have to be getting home," Gwen said.

"Oh, okay. Well, it was nice seeing you again. Thanks for your help in school today."

Gwen grinned. "You're welcome."

Several seconds of awkward silence passed.

"Well I guess I'll be going," she said.

Chris nodded as he yearned to return his attention to the cheerleaders.

"But my mom dropped me off, so I don't have a ride."

Chris was silent.

"I guess I could walk," she added.

Chris nodded.

"Maybe nothing will happen to me."

Chris finally picked up on the hint. "I'm sorry. Do you need a lift?"

"Sure," Gwen said. "If it's not too much trouble."

"No, of course not." Chris started to follow Gwen but took one last look back.

Roxy was still looking at him, smiling, as if knowing he was being taken away against his will.

CHAPTER TWO

———— ❈ ————

"Give me a C. Give me an A. Give me a V…"

Much to the annoyance of the crowd, the cheerleading squad continued until they had spelled out C-A-V-A-L-I-E-R-S.

The night after the first day of school for the students of Frenchtown High School was their customary time to hold the first pep rally of the year. After this one, the pep rallies would be held every Friday during school hours before each game. This year had a special feel to it. After all, this was supposed to be their year. Most of the starters of the football team were returning as seniors and it was hoped, or rather dreamed, that 1987 would be the year the Cavaliers would bring home their second state championship. The trophy from 1954 was still looking very lonely in the principal's office.

The night air was cool but still humid. There wasn't a cloud in the sky and, even with the lights around the field shouting down artificial rays of sunshine, the stars were still visible. Moths and other flying insects carried on their dizzying love affair with the stadium bulbs. The lone howl of a train could be heard in the distance. Dew drops dared to form on the tips of the grass even while everyone trampled around.

The football coach had already left after giving his best Knute Rockne impersonation where he rattled off the team's accomplishments, praised their hard work, exaggerated their skills, and finally called upon the gods to deliver this year's team to the state championship. He had never been comfortable speaking in front of large groups. Seriously, who is? But he knew it was his duty to support his players and do whatever he could to fire up the fans.

Most of the other teachers had left as well. About half of the student body remained. High schoolers all over the field intuitively congregated in tight-knit groups with those of like minds and pursuits: the jocks, the academics, the nerds, the tech geeks, the popular bunch, the outcasts, etc. Most seemed in no hurry to leave. Most seemed to care less about school spirit, and more about enjoying being anywhere but home.

Roxy loved the pep rallies. She loved everything to do with displaying support for her school and its teams. But right now her mind was far from those ideas. She kept scanning the faces in search of a certain one that she hoped had returned from his noble distraction. But the one face above all others she sought out was not to be seen. Like Chris, she had also been practicing for their first official meeting. She was sure they would have so much in common. She could see how his calm exterior radiated proof of his intellectual mind.

"Let's hear it, guys," Mannie Flarity shouted as he waved his pompoms and bounced up and down. Mannie was the only male cheerleader on the six-person team and could be best described as pretty. He wasn't very tall nor particularly athletic, but he had the rhythm to fit right in with the rest of them. His long, straight black hair reflected the towering lights around the football field and his slender frame made most of the girls jealous. His dark eyes turned many heads. His voice was barely a high-pitched whisper. To the jocks he was a delicate flower. But he had learned that the younger girls were drawn to this persona, to his sensitivity, so he milked it for all it was worth.

"Let's do a pyramid," Mannie instructed the five female cheerleaders. Mannie wore sweatpants instead of a skirt but with the same school insignia: a dark blue silhouette of a 17th century French swashbuckler's hat complete with flowered plume.

Some of the students made a circle around them to watch as each of the other cheerleaders readied to take their place in the scheme.

The ten members of the basketball team were there as well, and, like the majority of football players, wore their jerseys to show support for their school, or simply to show off. The cheerleaders pulled double duty between the football and basketball games.

Roxy acted as end support and got into her stance so another cheerleader could step up onto her thigh. Mannie made up the other corner. Another would then stand between them and, after that, two of the others would step up into place. The crucial part came when the smallest of them climbed up on the shoulders of the middle two. Thus the pyramid would be formed with three cheerleaders on the bottom row, two in the middle, and one on top.

Before it could begin, however…

"Hey, puny one. Get off the football field now. Did I not make myself clear at school today when I told you not to show your face here?"

Heads turned and whispers floated throughout the kids. Who had yelled such a thing?

"Didn't I tell you not to show up here tonight?" the voice rang out again.

Larry Dukes, whom everyone called "Cap" because he was the captain of the football team, shook his head. Cap was a senior this year, and, while not necessarily a handsome fellow, was one heck of a leader on the field. He was 5'10" with square everything: square shoulders, square hips, square jaw, and his high-and-tight haircut even made his head appear square. He looked over at Roger. "It's Cedric. Should've known he'd do something like this."

Roger Sims, who was now standing with Cap, looked around to see for himself. "Oh no," he whispered. Roger had heard Cedric present his warning to Mannie earlier in the day at school. He wasn't sure why Cedric had done such a thing, but he had secretly worried about it all day.

The crowd parted like the Red Sea as if an invisible person was pushing their way through the bodies and forcing them to take a step backward. A direct line from the cheerleaders slowly opened like the ground splitting during an earthquake. The widening line spread to reveal the source of the loud thundering voice.

There sat Cedric DeBurr on a huge plastic cooler, and he was indeed the largest football player this town had ever seen. He stood six feet and weighed in at just over 300 pounds and could bench press a small village. He had a round face and double chin. His hair was a reddish brown and looked like it had been cut using a warped broken bowl. His thick eyebrows almost went all the way across his huge head. He wore black sweatpants and a black sweatshirt, which was basically all he ever wore except in the summer when he wore black sweatshirts with the sleeves half cut off, or during a game when he wore his jersey. Unlike the other players, he cared not to wear his football jersey except when he was playing. He did not play football for acceptance, or to display his ability, or to show off, or even to help his school. For Cedric, it served as a release for pent-up aggression.

While most of Cedric's massive frame was muscle, he also had an unbelievably large midsection, which had earned him the nickname "Cedric the Bulge." That name was only whispered in private because anyone who merely mentioned his size, or anything perceived to reference his weight or shape, felt the blunt of Cedric's giant club-like fists and the force by which his giant arms could deliver them. Many students in the past had learned this the hard way and all knew now to make that the one subject not spoken around this teen behemoth.

"Why are you still here?" Cedric asked as his glare bore a hole right into Mannie.

Mannie turned to the basketball team. "Guys, a little help, please."

"Quiet down, Cedric," one of the players offered.

"Yeah, let them do their thing," another followed.

Yet another: "Show a little respect."

"Keep it up, fellows," Cedric said, "and you'll be dribbling for the rest of your lives, and not on the court but from the straw by which you'll be forced to feed."

No one from the basketball team uttered another word.

"Now, little one," he said once again directly addressing Mannie. "Where were we?"

But the masses weren't quite subdued just yet.

"Leave him alone," a student in the crowd shouted.

"Yeah, stop interrupting," another called out.

Other faceless heroes chimed in from the safety of the shadows.

"Mind your own business," Cedric yelled and stepped up on top of the cooler. Thank goodness it was well constructed. "I'll make you all an offer. Anyone who wishes to take his place and have my full attention, please step forward. If you wish to show everyone how brave and valiant you are, I can appreciate that. To show you how much I admire that, I promise not to break every bone in your bodies. So please come on up and form a line. Be the first and I'll make sure a shrine is constructed in your honor and displayed in the hallways of the school. Everyone will know you stood up for the cause. Everyone will send flowers to your hospital room. Who will be the first? Come show the entire school what you're made of. We shall rejoice in your bravery."

Silence.

"What?" Cedric asked as he looked around the crowd. "Surely there is one hero amongst you. What about you?" He pointed to a male student nearby.

The student quickly dropped his head.

"Ah, no. What about you?"

Another male student stood frozen.

"Not you either? Anyone?" Cedric bellowed out. "Anyone at all?"

Dead silence.

"Seriously? No one, huh? Then keep your mouths shut and do not interrupt me again." Cedric sat back on the cooler and turned his attention back to Mannie. "So, Mr. Cheerleader, are you still here?"

"I have every right to be here," Mannie countered weakly. "You are not the boss of me."

"Tell you what," Cedric said, "I'll count to three. A count helps put things into focus, into perspective. A count heightens awareness and anticipation, and anticipation can be far worse than the actual actions. And by actions, I of course refer to the beating coming. I'll count to three and if you're still here, I'll carry you off the field myself… in pieces.

"One…" Cedric held up his index finger.

"You don't scare me," Mannie said as he tried to keep his knees from buckling. "Try anything and everyone will come to my defense."

"Two…" Cedric raised both his index and middle finger.

"This is a free country. I can do whatever I want. There isn't a force on Earth that can move me from this spot."

"Three."

The crowd erupted in laughter as Mannie was

halfway across the field before his pompoms hit the ground.

Cedric smiled but it quickly disappeared.

Miss Andrews did not laugh. She was a young teacher, plain but pretty, and the cheerleading coach. "Cedric, why do you pick on Mannie? You should be ashamed of yourself. He's a wonderful person and a great cheerleader."

"I have my reasons," Cedric said earnestly. "First, he's a horrible cheerleader and only does it to be close to the cutest girls in school. He is crude and clumsy and moans his cheers much like a dog begs for a bone. Second… Well, that reason is for me to know alone."

"What am I going to do with you?" Miss Andrews asked. "I suppose you want to take his place in the pyramid now?"

Cedric laughed and shook his head. "No, not me."

"Well, I was very much looking forward to the pyramid, so I suppose you owe me and the others who wanted to see it an apology."

"Indeed you are correct, my dear Miss Andrews." Cedric stood and turned in a circle while speaking. "I apologize to all, and hope you enjoy the rest of the evening."

"Thank you." Miss Andrews couldn't get too upset with Cedric. After all, she was also the sponsor of the math team, and, besides being the toughest guy in the school, Cedric was also the star of the math team and had helped them win two first-place trophies the previous year, a feat the school had never before accomplished. In fact, they had never even placed.

The football players loved when Cedric became loud and boisterous, and several made their way over to show their admiration. They circled around him and heaped praise upon his actions.

Not everyone, however, was a fan. Among the onlookers was another student, one who despised Cedric with a passion: Anthony Royal. Anthony's dad was the mayor of Frenchtown and they had money, family money, and Anthony was quite at ease showing it off. They also owned the hometown newspaper, the *Frenchtown Gazette*. He proudly drove around town in a Ferrari like the one on *Magnum P.I.* Anthony was the epitome of tall, dark, and handsome. His thick dark hair came down low on his brow and ended with a widow's peak. He was built quite well, though he looked down on people who played sports. In fact, he looked down on almost everyone. His expensive designer clothes complemented his Rolex and solid gold class ring.

He stood beside Roxy and Madison Gilbert, another cheerleader and Roxy's best friend. Anthony was very attracted to Roxy and had been for a long time, but so far his advances had proven futile. It wasn't for lack of trying. He was always purchasing small gifts for her, even though she objected each time, and would ask her out almost every weekend. As if expecting her to say no each time, he always had another girl on standby.

"Who is this jerk?" Ty Victor asked. Ty went to another school in the same county and was a longtime friend of Anthony's. Ty was well known in the annals of high school lore for his many Karate titles. Although he was not quite as tall and muscular as Anthony, his trim physique and short dark hair made him look like a Hollywood action star. He fancied himself as such also.

"That's Cedric," Roxy answered as she brushed her thick blond bangs from her beautiful face.

"He's a smart aleck," Anthony said. "He's always been a smart aleck."

"I don't know about 'aleck,'" Roxy said, "but he is the smartest person in our class and the best football player, and the best fighter in the entire state."

Ty took issue with that last part, especially since he knew himself to be the best.

So did Anthony. "I believe that distinction goes to my friend Ty here."

"So," Ty asked, "why does he stuff his shirt? Is that like a pillow or something?"

Madison's mouth dropped open.

"No, it's not," Roxy said with words clear and firm. "And just some advice: don't say anything like that to him." She and Madison walked away and rejoined the other cheerleaders.

Cap, shaking his head in disapproval, walked over to Cedric.

Cedric chuckled, knowing his friend didn't approve. All of the football players looked up to Cedric, but Cap was the only one he thought of as a real friend.

"Are you having fun?" Cap asked.

"I am indeed, my friend."

"You'll never change, will you?"

"Let us hope not," Cedric answered.

Cap laughed.

"Excuse me," a student said as he walked up. "Cedric, right?"

Cedric looked the boy over. He had seen him before but wasn't sure who he was. He was skinny with sunken eyes and bony nose.

"I'm Matt. I work with Roger on the school paper," the boy explained as if knowing he wasn't recognized. "I'm doing a story on school bullies and was wondering if I could interview you."

"Sorry," Cedric said. "I don't know any."

"None?" the boy asked with a wry smile.

"That's what I said."

The boy started scribbling on a notepad as if Cedric had agreed and was now conducting the interview. "Would you call yourself an angry person?"

"No, but I'm getting there fast."

The boy stopped writing and looked up at Cedric. "Well. I was just wondering…"

"You are dismissed," Cedric said.

"But…"

"I said you are dismissed. Now run along."

Then the boy made a mistake. His eyes drifted downward.

"Why don't you go away?" Cedric asked then noticed the focus of the boy's attention. "Wait a minute. Are you staring at my belly?"

The boy looked up quickly. "No. I uh…"

"Why not?" Cedric asked. "Go ahead if you're so curious; take a good look."

"I didn't look," the boy said, his voice breaking up a bit. "I made sure not to look."

"Oh really? Why not? Does it bother you?" Cedric walked up close, his huge stomach mere inches from the boy. "Does the shape seem odd to you? Does it gross you out? Maybe you find it just a tad large."

"No, not at all. I would say small even."

"What? Are you blind?" Cedric snapped. Grabbing the boy by the shoulder, he pulled him in close. "That's an insult. Don't you know that a huge midsection is a sign of success? I happen to be very proud of that. I cherish this belly of mine. It commands admiration, astonishment, and respect. It embodies that which makes a man great, a superior specimen, and a true legend. But look at you. You're a runt, a thin, puny, skinny, unsuccessful runt. Your torso is as devoid of substance as your intellect. That worthless concavity that joins your hips to your sunken chest is a disgrace. Now get out of here before I break you in half."

When he let go of his shoulder the boy fell back on his rear, but hopped up and ran away as fast as he could.

The people in viewing distance laughed at the clumsy exit.

"You're absolutely crazy," Cap said. "Have you ever thought of being friendly to people?"

Cedric laughed. "I have all the friends I will ever need."

Cap shook his head. "You can never have too many friends. Just think, you'll need at least six one day. Who do you think will carry your casket?"

"I don't know," Cedric said as if seriously pondering the humorous question. "But I hope they're pretty strong."

CHAPTER THREE

———◆◆◆———

Cap and Cedric continued their discussion as did everyone else. About half the people had left the pep rally. Small circles of students checkered the green grass, shadows being cast in all directions from the towering lights for each one.

Cap walked away to speak to some other football players leaving Cedric standing there like a lone oak tree. Cedric stared into the darkness surrounding the lit area of the field with his hands crossed in front of his massive chest. He breathed deeply through his nose and took in the aroma of the night. He was neither at peace nor tormented. He simply stood staring as if this entire town was his domain. The shenanigans of the evening seemed to be over and attentions drifted away from him for the moment, and for the moment he was content.

Anthony and Ty were still there. Like Anthony, Ty came from a wealthy family and dressed in expensive clothes and shoes, and drove a fancy sports car. He thought of himself as not only a great fighter, but as a most sought-after lady's-man as well. Unfortunately, he also thought of himself as the righter of wrongs, the champion of the oppressed, and the beacon of all things that needed illumination.

"This guy's a big blowhard," Ty said as they still watched from a distance. It was clear that Cedric's antics had annoyed him greatly. He kept staring as if hoping someone would avenge the poor male cheerleader and do something. Of course no one did.

A devious grin crept across Anthony's face as his thoughts teased him. "Maybe someone should put him in his place."

"All right," Ty said. "I will."

Anthony smiled as his suggestion took root.

Ty walked toward the huge savage who needed to be taught a lesson. No, it would be safer to say he strolled, like a person who was invulnerable to anything or anyone. After all, that's what his parents, his Karate instructor, and life had taught him. He had not a worry in the world as he approached Cedric and looked him over. Then with a flash of genius, he delivered his masterpiece. "Hey, fatso."

The night grew silent. Deafly silent. It was as if air raid sirens had instigated a blackout and enemy planes were flying overhead. No one dared take a step or utter a word. It seemed even the crickets sensed the danger and halted their incessant chirping. Every student froze, only their neck muscles working as all heads slowly spun around to witness the tragedy apparent, each wondering if they had heard what they thought they had heard. Had someone been so foolish as to speak this blasphemy? The tension that filled the air was as real and present as the humidity itself.

Seconds passed as Cedric looked over his insulter. "'Fatso'? Seriously?" he finally asked and shook his head.

"That's it? That's all you got?"

"Well," Ty countered, "I mean I could—"

"No, no, no," Cedric said as he pointed to his belly with both hands. "You have this to work with and that lame phrase is all you can come up with? Why would you waste an opportunity like this? "

"Well, let me think," Ty said.

"Don't do that. It's clear you don't know how. It's obvious that your mental acuity lacks even the basic abilities afforded a Kindergartener. Seriously, if a meteorite the size of Rhode Island was to land on your house, would you say, 'Look at that gravel'? Would you compare Godzilla to a tapeworm? Would you call the Titanic a rowboat or the iceberg it hit an ice cube? If you're going to make a grandstand, then go all out. Don't cower behind small comparisons."

"I suppose you could come up with something better?" Ty asked.

A slow smile crept across Cedric's large face. "Oh, I think I'm up to that challenge, little man. Let me tell you some things you could have said if you didn't ride the short bus to school."

The crowd once again paid attention and Cedric loved it. Everyone gathered around and listened closely.

Cedric walked closer to his adversary and spoke loudly.

"Clothing:

"What is your belt size, the equator?

"Medical:

"When you were born and the doctor slapped you, did you eat him?

"Dietary:

"You know you're supposed to pick only one thing from the menu, right?

"Rescue:

"I bet they used the Jaws of Life to deliver you.

"Fashion:

"Where do you shop, the big and tall hot-air balloon store?

"Geology:

"Do you have your own zip code?

"Anatomy:

"When was the last time you saw your feet?

"Shipping:

"Do you get your mail at Taco Bell?

"Science:

"And I thought there were only nine planets.

"Vacation:

"When you lie down on the beach, do people come and try to roll you back into the water?

"Stock Market:

"I'm guessing Krispy Kreme shares are soaring.

"Cuisine:

"Did you ever meet a pizza you didn't like?

"Marketing:

"Hammock for sale, crane sold separately.

"Complimentary:

"You're such a nice guy to make the circus elephants feel at home."

The crowd giggled, chuckled, and sometimes howled at each colorful insult.

"These are some things you could have said," Cedric added, "if you weren't a moron with the mind of a child. But having not one bit of wit, not one ounce of originality, not one iota of cleverness, and not one atom of courage emanating from any bone in your pathetic body, you never had a chance. Of all the syllables you could have strung together to make a successful insult, you failed and only need one to sum you up — prick."

Perhaps sensing the situation was reaching the point of no return, Anthony rushed up behind Ty. "Come on, let's go. It's not worth it." He tugged at Ty's shoulder hoping to persuade his friend to follow.

"Yes, run along," Cedric said with a wry smile. "Show everyone you're not just a mental midget, but a coward as well."

But Ty wasn't finished. He couldn't walk away now. He was insulted and had to get the last word. "Look at this freak. Who dresses you? You're like a giant alien slob."

The tension grew tenser.

"That is true," Cedric said. "My mommy and daddy do not buy me pretty little clothes and fancy little shoes so I can pretend to be a real man. Real men are known by their intellect, by their courage, and by their actions. A real man stands by his words with fortitude, integrity, and pride. A real man is revealed from what's in his heart, not like cowards who disguise their insecurities behind cute little threads that hide their puny bodies and puny souls. In other words, a real man wouldn't stand there talking like a frightened little boy, shaking in their two-hundred-dollar sneakers like you are currently doing."

"That's it. Let's go, you lard butt." Ty got into his Karate stance to show he was ready to fight.

Cedric grinned. His taunting had paid off. Of course he knew this would be the inevitable outcome. This person had committed the cardinal sin and had to pay the price. Cedric would have chased him down if necessary. "You got it, son. This is going to be fun."

Ty smirked. "Oh, you're a poet and don't know it."

"Actually I do know it, so here's what I will do. As I kick your puny ass, I'll make up a poem just for you. But when the rhymes are over, it's lights out."

"Is that right?" Ty asked still in his stance.

Cedric's smile disappeared. "It is."

An eerie silence fell over the remaining students still on the ballfield. The crowd and Anthony backed away and made a huge circle to give them room.

Cedric closed his eyes to create his poetry. He moved his hands back and forth in the air much like a conductor orchestrating a symphony. "I am ready," he said as he opened his eyes. "The Battle Between Deburr and a Simpleton."

"What do you mean by that remark?" Ty asked.

Cedric smiled. "That's the title of my poem, moron."

Everyone laughed.

Both of the men prepared, but Cedric did not even lift his fists as he began his improvisation.

"Come, on, pretty boy with your fancy martial arts,

"With hair that smells of flowers and breath that reeks of farts.

"Your story is a sad one, but one that must be told

"So it begins; let's get this show on the road"

"Oohs" and "awws" echoed throughout the bystanders.

Ty rushed him and leapt into the air and twisted in a complete circle. He wasted no time and went for his most deadly move: the spinning roundhouse kick. It landed right where it was aimed: square in the middle of his opponent's chest. This same move had devastated opponents in his Karate class and won him several points and even victories during full-contact tournaments.

Cedric didn't budge at all.

Ty backed away in astonishment.

"Now's the time to be reflective

"Knowing your skills are ineffective

"You're no champion, but rather a clown

"But it's too late to turn back now"

Ty swung with a roundhouse right then a roundhouse left. Cedric blocked them both easily with his huge arms. Ty tried uppercuts, jabs, crosses, and kicks. Nothing worked. Most were easily blocks and the blows that did land had zero effect.

The crowd formed a huge circle around them as several cheered for Cedric, the football players especially.

Roxy stood with Madison and looked on in fear,

her breathing escalated, and her hand at her neck. Madison held onto Roxy's shoulders to comfort her. Roxy hated confrontation and despised violence. The night air suddenly seemed to get colder as she shivered in her cheerleading outfit.

When Ty's attacks using his feet and fist failed, he began swinging wildly. He apparently now realized the gravity of the situation and the seriousness of his predicament. The realization was made worse with the knowledge that he had brought this on his self.

Cedric blocked each swing, but drifted backward as Ty continued this bombardment. The onlookers gave way as Cedric backpedaled through the damp grass and backed all the way up to the chain-link fence that separated the field from the bleachers.

Ty began to tire and gasped for breath.

"He swings away like a Neanderthal man
"Much like General Custard and his last stand
"A mistake has been made, a tough lesson to learn
"But it's too late now, because it's my turn"

Cedric began swinging round his huge right arm in surprising swiftness. Ty was able to throw up both arms in front of his face, in a crossbones formation, to block each punch, but the mere force of each blow drove him backward — way backward.

Once again the crowd gave way as the two combatants now went all the way across to the other sideline until Ty's back was again the fence on that side.

Cedric launched lefts and rights at his opponent's

face. As Ty was able to block these punches, Cedric suddenly switched to his abdomen, landing blows that drove the remaining air from Ty's lungs.

Ty tried hard to breathe.

"The end is near, no ifs, ands, or butts
"Next time you'll know to keep your big mouth shut
"You'll look like a coward and sound like a wimp
"But it's better than walking forever with a limp"

It was clear that Cedric's lyrics were getting on Ty's nerves, which is probably why Cedric continued to talk and to swing. A blow finally landed on the side of Ty's head, causing him to become temporarily disoriented and his arms to drop by his side. At that moment he was entirely defenseless. Cedric eased up and waited. He reached down and lifted Ty's fists back up into a protective posture.

"Now you see your challenge has been met
"But it's not over so don't quit on me yet
"Summon the power of the moon and the sun
"Let's not stop because this is too much fun."

Ty shook the cobwebs from his mind and, with his back against the fence, threw a desperation shot with his right fist. Cedric caught it and held it in his left hand, squeezing Ty's fist until the blood rushed from the flesh. Ty threw his left and Cedric caught it in his right hand and held firm. This left Ty completely vulnerable.

"Now in the end do you finally understand"

Cedric thrust his large midsection into Ty, ramming him hard against the fence.

"What happens when a boy takes on a man"

Cedric thrust again.

"But the rhymes are finished; it's the end of our bout"

Another thrust.

"And like I promised you; now it's lights out."

In a lightning-fast move, Cedric let go of Ty's left hand and delivered a right uppercut to Ty's unsuspecting chin. The force of the blow lifted Ty's feet a full foot off the ground and it almost appeared as he would flip right over the fence. But as Cedric backed away, he fell forward to the ground like a sack of potatoes, and lay just as unanimated. His face landed hard on the dew-tainted sod and he lay there like a ragdoll. He was out cold.

The students cheered.

Anthony rushed to his friend's side and tried to wake him by slapping his cheeks. It didn't work. "Help me here," he called out to anyone.

Several guys sat Ty up in a seated position and then hoisted him off the ground. They then followed

Anthony toward the parking lot.

Cedric watched as they left. His face showed neither sadness nor triumph. In fact, he was stoic, indifferent, and emotionally numb.

Some of the football players came up to congratulate Cedric on his victory. But the pep rally was over and the crowd, including the jubilant football players, started thinning out as everyone headed home.

Cedric retook his seat on the large cooler.

"You're an idiot," Cap said. "If any of the teachers had still been here, you could have been suspended… or worse."

Cedric simply smiled.

"Why can't you just be normal?"

Cedric smirked. "Why on Earth would anyone aspire to be normal? Is that really what you wish of me? Would you be content if I was just a regular person? Please let me know how to become the person you wish me to be and I shall try my utmost."

"Fine," Cap said. "You've made your point. But do you have to attack everyone? Now the entire basketball team hates you. Mannie hates you. Anthony hates you. I'm sure that Ty fellow, who probably has a broken jaw, will never love you. How many people hating you is enough?"

"It's never enough."

Cap shook his head. "You should be more like me. I don't make waves. I just go with the flow. I believe we should all walk the straight line."

"The straight line?" Cedric asked. "The straight line is in the middle of the road and the most dangerous place to walk. Where has that approach ever gotten you, my friend?"

"Nowhere," Cap admitted. "I'll probably end up with some dead-end job, a mobile home, eight kids, and bills out the wazoo."

Cedric laughed. "But you won't be hated, right?"

"Exactly," Cap said with a chuckle. "Come on. Let's go to the Frosty Freeze and get a burger."

"Not I."

"Why not?"

Cedric turned out the pockets in his sweat pants. "I don't have any money."

Cap understood. Cedric never had money. He lived with his mom, who was an older lady and disabled. No one ever knew what happened to his father. Playing football and being on the math team didn't allow Cedric to leave school early for a job, so he got by anyway he could. Most days at school he didn't even have lunch money. Many times he sat with the other football players in the lunchroom with nothing to eat at all. He qualified for free lunches but his pride would not allow him to accept charity, so he never applied.

"Excuse me, sir."

Cedric and Cap looked at the girl who had walked up. She was very cute but small for a high school student, probably a freshman. Her brown hair came only to her shoulders. Her hazel-colored eyes peered out from evenly-cut bangs. She wore jeans and a purple sweater. She simply stood there waiting.

"Can I help you?" Cedric asked.

The girl pointed to the cooler, her index finger

shaking a little. "That's our cooler, the band I mean. They sent me to retrieve it. But if you're still using it…"

"Oh," Cedric said and stood up. "I'm sorry, sweetie. Here, please take it. I'm sorry I was keeping it from you."

The girl nodded and grabbed the handle on one side and began to pull the cooler away. But then she stopped. "Sorry. I couldn't help but overhear your conversation. I hate you don't have money to eat. I think we have a lot left over." She lifted the lid on the cooler and took out a sandwich in a sealed bag, a bag of chips, and a soda and held them out to Cedric.

Cedric smiled. "That's very sweet, but I cannot accept."

The girl looked very sad.

"Now don't look like that," Cedric said. "Okay, if it causes you pain for me to refuse, I will take the chips and soda. Thank you very much."

The girl looked into the cooler. "Don't you want anything else?"

"Yes I do; the name of the beautiful princess who rescued me."

The girl blushed and smiled. "I'm Cindy."

Cedric took her small hand in his giant one and kissed it gently.

Cindy giggled then hurried away, cooler in tow.

"Moron," Cap said.

Cedric laughed. "Hey, got me a free snack." He quickly devoured the chips and soda. "Ah, that really hit the spot. I tell you, Cap, I was starving."

They both laughed.

CHAPTER FOUR

"Can I ask you something?" Cap asked.

"Anything," Cedric said and was being honest.

"What have you got against Mannie? He's an alright guy."

Cedric shrugged. "I just hate the whole idea of male cheerleaders."

"I don't believe that for a second." Cap said. "Heck, if you could fit into one of those outfits, you'd probably be a cheerleader yourself."

Cedric laughed at the thought of himself in a cheerleader outfit. That would give the kids nightmares. But he also knew Cap might be right. He was definitely a man of the 80s believing a boy could do almost anything a girl could do.

"Come on now," Cap said, "tell me the real reason."

Cedric paused as if wondering whether to open up about it. Finally he shook his head and began. "He's a wimp but he acts like he can bench press five hundred pounds. He struts around school like a superhero or something. He considers himself God's gift to women. He stares at them with those sad pathetic eyes, crying over the least little thing, and they eat it up. I've never understood the fairer sex, but how can anyone be attracted to weakness? I hate him ever since he set his sights upon…"

Cedric stopped midsentence but Cap had gotten the gist, and it took him by surprise. He had to wrap his mind around this new revelation before he could speak. "Wait a minute. Are you saying what I think you're saying? Have you been bitten by the love bug? Is it even possible?"

Cedric looked at his friend and nodded. "It is possible. I have been bitten and I am smitten."

"This is huge," Cap said with the tips of his fingers touching both sides of his head. In all the years he had known him, which had basically been since Kindergarten when Cedric beat him up for saying "fat" in his presence, Cedric had never even talked about girls. "Will you tell me who it is?"

Cedric crossed his arms across his chest. "Who do you think? I mean, look at me. Look at this body. The ugliest, homeliest girls in this school would run from me like I was a giant alien bug with six-feet-long pinchers and a ten-feet-long stinging tail. Who would I have the audacity to fall head-over-heels for? Why of course I would have to fall for the most beautiful girl in the school."

"Most beautiful?" Cap asked. "Wait a minute. Is it Roxy?"

Cedric looked at his friend solemnly and nodded. "It is Roxy."

"That's wonderful," Cap said. "Sure, why not? Ask her out."

"Get real. Look at this body. It's hopeless."

"Why?" Cap asked. "Why can't it work out for you?"

Cedric sighed. "Sometimes I think I could have someone. One night I was walking to the gym and noticed a couple in each other's arms sitting on one of the benches in the park. They seemed so happy. It's as if they knew a secret language all their own and nobody but them could speak or understand it. I stared for several minutes before moving on. When I got to the gym, there was a couple sitting in the corner laughing with each other in yet another foreign tongue. And for a moment I forgot. For a moment I thought I could do that too. I could love and be loved. I could hold someone's heart as my own and be as one and speak in our own private code. But then I saw my reflection in the mirror and it brought me back to reality." Cedric clinched his fist and pounded his thigh.

"But you have so much more to offer. Not every girl you meet is hung up on physical appearance."

"No, my friend," Cedric said. "I dare not dream anymore. There is no hope for me or for this monstrosity beneath my chest that arrives everywhere fifteen minutes before I do."

Cap didn't know what to say. He knew his friend was hurting but he didn't have the medicine to fix it.

"I'm sorry," Cedric said seeing the saddened look in Cap's eyes. "You don't need to hear this. You have better things to do than take on this charity case. I'm just bitter knowing myself so fat and so alone."

Cap smiled. "But why alone? I truly believe there's

a girl for every guy. Hey, that cute little girl who just offered you food did not run screaming from you."

Cedric's brow lowered as he looked in the direction the girl had walked away. "No, she didn't, did she?'

"Well, Roxy too."

Cedric quickly looked at Cap, his eyes wide open. "What does that mean?"

"She watched your fight," Cap said. "And I could tell she was nervous. She had one hand up like this." Cap acted out the charade. "I think she was biting her fingernails."

"Really?" Cedric's eyes took on a glimmer of hope.

"And I'm certain it wasn't the other guy she was worried about. I'm serious. Ask her out, dude. Take a chance. Look at it this way, the worst that can happen is she will say no. Then you're in exactly the same place. Hey, nothing ventured, nothing gained I always say."

The idea started to take root as Cedric almost began to believe there was a chance. Just a chance. But it just as quickly disappeared. "No, that's not the worst that can happen, not the worst by far. She could laugh at me. That thought scares me more than a thousand alien bugs."

Before Cap could respond, he saw someone approaching and motioned to Cedric. Cedric turned to look and saw another cheerleader walking toward them.

"Madison," Cedric whispered.

"Hey guys," she said as she walked up. She still wore her cheerleader skirt but had on someone's letterman jacket. She was smiling a devious smile, the look of someone with juicy gossip.

"Madison," Cedric and Cap both said.

Madison's smile grew wider. "Cedric, someone wanted me to ask you if you were free for lunch tomorrow."

"Someone?" Cedric asked.

Madison laughed. "You know who I mean. Roxy wanted me to ask you if you could meet her for lunch tomorrow at the Frosty Freeze."

Cedric was dumbstruck.

"She needs to talk to you about something important," Madison added in his silence.

Cedric finally found his voice. "Uh, yeah, I can be there. Tell her I'll be there."

"Okay, I'll let her know." Madison smiled again and walked away.

"Oh my God!" Cedric said. "She wants to talk to me. Did you hear that? She wants to talk to me."

"Not so morbid anymore I see."

Cedric shook his head in confusion. "Well at least she knows I'm alive."

Cap laughed. "That's always a good thing. Your spirits have lifted. Good for you."

"Are you kidding me?" Cedric joked. "I am ecstatic. My head is getting dizzy. I feel like Hercules. I think I could take on the Dallas Cowboys right now. Heck, put Zeus and Apollo in pads and helmets and bring them on. I am on fire right now. Where there was once darkness, there is now light."

As soon as he finished that sentence, the field lights went off, leaving them in almost complete darkness.

Cedric and Cap laughed at the irony. They hadn't even realized they were the last two students remaining after the pep rally.

"I think that's our cue," Cap said.

"Indeed," Cedric said. "Let's go. What an incredible night."

Before they could get completely off the field, however, they were stopped. Cedric's night was far from over.

"Cedric! Cedric!" Roger Sims came running up out of breath.

"What is it?" Cedric asked.

"Let me go home with you tonight."

"What's the problem?" Cap asked.

Roger looked back in the direction he had just came then back at Cap and Cedric. "Remember that story I wrote about the mayor for the school paper?"

Cedric laughed. He obviously remembered.

"Well," Roger continued, "Anthony was really upset. He took the story seriously and told some others I was spreading rumors about his dad. Then I heard others were upset too. Now someone has gotten a dozen men to beat me up. They're waiting for me now."

Cap shook his head. "Come on. That was what, three months ago? You don't actually believe people are still upset enough about that to really do something, do you?"

"Not at first, but I was just walking home and there was a group of men and I'm certain they were waiting for me. I'm pretty sure they were waiting to beat me up."

Cap and Cedric looked at each other. They knew Roger only lived about half a mile from the school.

"You're going home tonight, Roger," Cedric said. "I'll walk you myself."

"Are you crazy?" Cap asked. "A dozen grown men?"

"Sounds fair to me," Cedric answered. He was still electrified from Madison's news.

"Come here," Cap said waving his hand. When Cedric was beside him, he whispered, "You're going to risk your butt for Roger?"

Cedric looked at Roger before looking back to Cap. "I like Roger. I consider him a good friend. He's on the math team with me and he's a great writer. But there's a more important reason."

"What?" Cap asked.

"If Roger gets beaten up tonight, he might end up in the hospital. And if that happens, his family will be there with him. That means that tomorrow at lunch the Frosty Freeze will be closed, and I can't risk that."

Cap stood there befuddled as Cedric walked away with Roger. Soon they were out of sight, but Cap followed at a distance.

As Cedric and Roger left the football field, the street lights in front of the school guided their trek. Then the moon took over to provide dim illumination as the two high school seniors got farther from the street lights surrounding the school building. And the farther they walked, the more nervous Roger became. He stayed right behind Cedric.

"Maybe we should go back," he said as he stopped and looked back at the schoolhouse, no doubt missing the safety it provided. But when he looked back, he noticed Cedric had continued onward, so he quickly caught up to him. "I shouldn't have written those jokes," he added.

Cedric stopped and turned around. "Of course you shouldn't have. What in the world were you thinking? I mean, freedom to express your thoughts is a stupid thing for citizens of a free republic to possess. It's basically destroying the fabric of our society. Why, we should completely eliminate the entire First Amendment altogether. Heck, why don't we just give communism a try? How does that sound?"

The sarcasm did not go undetected as Roger smiled and nodded. He knew Cedric was right, but right now fear was in control of his logic.

They continued onward. Cedric began to whistle to break the tension. As they neared the edge of the school property where it met the residential road that led to Roger's house, the old saw mill came into view. It was a cinderblock building, about fifty years old, and was an empty shell with the roof having fallen in years ago. When they were only a dozen feet away, a man stepped out of the dilapidated structure.

Cedric stopped whistling and looked him over but did not recognize him. He appeared to be a homeless wino. He did not look threatening at all. In fact, to Cedric, it looked like a stiff wind would blow him over. He wore extremely worn jeans and a flannel shirt missing at least three buttons with no t-shirt underneath. His scraggly chin went well past a five o'clock shadow and coarse black and white hair protruded in all directions. Cedric began to believe it was just a bum looking for change and not there for Roger. But then another like individual appeared. Then another.

Roger peeked out from behind Cedric, who simply stood there motionless staring at the gloomy trio. Several seconds of silence passed.

"We got no beef with you," the first man finally said to Cedric. "Just go on your way. Our dealings are between us and the boy behind you."

Cedric smiled. "No, my good man, it is *I* who is between you and the boy behind me."

The three men looked at each other. This was clearly not the mission for which they had agreed to undertake. More time passed as all five of them stayed exactly where they stood.

Another of the men spoke. "This ain't your business now. Just go back to the school and let us do what we came here to do."

"You didn't say the magic word," Cedric said.

All three guys breathed a sigh of relief and all three sang out in unison. "Please."

Cedric laughed. "Sorry, that's not the magic word."

There was no doubt left as to what was about to happen.

"So be it," the first wino responded and charged Cedric. He must have needed a drink pretty badly and figured if he didn't at least try, he wouldn't get his fistful of dollars.

Cedric simply stood there as the man approached while drawing back his fist. It seemed almost in slow motion as Cedric easily blocked the punch and grabbed the fellow around his thin right bicep. Just as quickly he grabbed the left bicep with his huge right hand and held the guy with little effort.

The other two looked on as their friend struggled to free himself but to no avail.

Cedric towered over him. He looked into the man's bloodshot eyes. "I'm going to give you guys one chance to walk away. I suggest you take it."

The others stayed put as the one in his grasp continued to resist.

"Don't say I didn't offer," Cedric said. He looked at the guy in front of him. "I'm sorry but this is probably going to sting a little."

Before the man could react, Cedric drew his body back and head-butted him right in the face causing him to hit the ground hard, blood gushing from a huge gash across the bridge of his nose.

The man screamed out in agony, piercing the stillness of the peaceful night.

Cedric stepped over him and looked at the two remaining.

The two others looked at each other and then to the darkness behind the old mill. Two other men stepped out into the moonlight. All four held their fists in front of their chests and slowly approached.

The first one that charged became a weapon as Cedric grabbed him around the neck with one hand, between the legs with the other, lifted him up, and threw him at the others. From there it became a free-for-all as they all came in with arms wailing away.

Cedric grabbed one around the neck, punched past him and landed his mighty fist on the guy behind him. That guy hit the ground hard, flipped over on his hands and knees, and scampered a few feet away before attempting to get back up.

When another threw a punch, Cedric moved the head of the guy whose neck he currently had in a death grip and let the blow land on him. Then Cedric swung round his colossal arm like a sledgehammer, hitting the guy who was fighting to breathe on top of the head and driving him to the ground like a spike.

Roger decided to hide behind the trunk of a large oak tree and watched from a distance. He thought of running to get help, but wasn't sure he would find anyone. Plus, he didn't want any of the men to chase him, catch him, and do to him what Cedric was doing to them.

The five would-be assailants regrouped and stood side-by-side, raised their feeble fists, and began to once again slowly approach.

"You have to be kidding me," Cedric said. "Well, come on. I can do this all night."

The weary quintuplet swallowed hard and came back for more. And more they got.

Cedric was through playing around. From that moment on he didn't hold back, and each bone-jarring punch connected with his full force. Each time a man went down this time, he did not immediately get back up.

They were more motivated than Cedric could

have predicted. It became comical as one-by-one they rushed in and tried to throw serious punches, but the punches got weaker and frailer with each attempt. And each time one punch from Cedric sent them reeling backward to the ground.

Cedric stood tall and drew in a deep breath as the five men all lay on the ground in front of him, some trying to get up while others seem to question if they should. He scanned the dark landscape expecting more men to come from the shadows but none ever did. "I have been cheated," he said, keeping a close eye on his foes. "Where are the dozen men I was promised?"

This thought seemed to enrage Cedric more as he beat the five men mercilessly until they were all bloodied, bruised, and refusing to get up and take any more punishment. Cedric stopped when they begged him to and he watched as they held onto each other and limped away.

Cedric exhaled the toxic fumes of anger and tried to calm down. He looked at his bloody fists and tilted his neck side-to-side to ease some of the pain where a few blows had landed on his own face.

Cap walked up behind him. "Happy now?" he asked.

Cedric laughed. "Well, pleasantly satisfied anyway. Come, let's go. I need a Diet Coke."

They started to walk away, but Cap stopped. "Where's Roger?"

Cedric's eyes got big. "Oh shoot. I almost forgot. Roger where are you?"

Roger finally stepped out from behind the tree.

"Is it clear?"

"All clear," Cedric said.

Roger joined his friends. Noticing a shoe and blood on the ground, he almost fainted. Cap and Cedric caught him and helped him make it home.

CHAPTER FIVE

———◆❖◆———

"Hey, son."

Anthony Royal looked up from the breakfast table to see his dad, the mayor. He was spent physically and emotionally stemming from the events of the previous night. "Hey, Dad."

The mayor took a seat at the table and picked up a piece of toast and smeared a little butter on it. The breakfast table sat in a large bay area beside the kitchen. It was beautifully decorated, as was the entire house, which was itself a showplace in the small town.

He wore pajamas and sported a morning shadow, which would be dutifully shaved away right after he ate. He was tall and lean and still had all his hair, though the areas above his ears were beginning to show strands of gray. After taking a bite, he looked across the table to his son. "I understand there was a disturbance at the pep rally last night, and an even bigger one after it. You know it doesn't look good on a mayor, especially a mayor who tries to promote Frenchtown as a friendly community."

Anthony got angry again just thinking about it. "It was that impossible hotheaded jock, Deburr."

"Yes, impossible," his dad echoed.

"The way he just disrupted the pep rally," Anthony said.

"Amazing."

"The way he treated poor Mannie."

"Deplorable."

"And what he did to my friend Ty."

"Crazy."

Anthony was getting worked up.

"How is your friend?" his dad asked.

"I took him to the emergency room last night. He has a chipped tooth and lots of bruises, and a mild concussion, but they say he will be alright."

"That's good."

"What will you do, Dad?"

"Nothing," the mayor answered. "I understand your friend Cedric was involved."

"He's not my friend," Anthony snapped. "If you know it was him, why don't you have him arrested?"

The mayor smiled. "I've always believed in the old motto that an ounce of prevention is worth a pound of cure. So maybe the question is: why didn't you keep it from happening?"

"I can't control that fat jerk. You could put him in jail."

"And what would that solve?" the mayor asked. "I know you don't care about football, and that breaks my heart, but because of Cedric we have a shot at a title again. That's a pretty big deal. We haven't even been to the playoffs in over a decade. This means so much to so many. If I were to put him in jail for having a simple schoolyard scuffle, the townsfolk would hang me out to dry."

"That's it?" Anthony asked. "That's why you won't punish him? You're afraid come November you'll be voted out of office?"

"No," the mayor said. "That's not the reason. Well, yes, I always worry about losing votes, but that has nothing to do with my stance on this subject. Do you have any idea what Cedric's life is like? Have you ever stopped to consider that? His dad left them when he was a baby. His mom is now disabled and they live off a tiny government check. Their house is barely larger than your bedroom. If you're ever going to be a leader in life, son, you better learn some empathy for those who are not as lucky or blessed as you."

Anthony swallowed his pride and nodded. "So what do you want me to do?"

"I understand he's quite a good writer. Let's get him to submit some articles for the newspaper and maybe we can put him on payroll."

"Are you serious?"

The mayor smiled. "I am dead serious. Maybe if we could keep him busy writing, he would have less time for fisticuffs. Does that not make sense to you?"

It was clear Anthony hated that idea, but he would do it for his father. "Okay, Dad, I'll talk with him." He finished eating his breakfast, got up, and nodded to his father as he left.

***

"Come away from the window, my friend. Sit and I'll bring you something to eat."

Cedric looked around and shook his head. "I don't have any money." He returned his attention to the parking area, closely eyeing every car that drove around the square.

Roger laughed. "Your money's no good here. What do you want, a burger? I can make you a pizza also. You need to eat."

Cedric didn't even hear the offer as he looked at the clock on the wall. It read 12:05. "Why did we just say 'lunch'? That can be anytime. She's not coming." He was already uncomfortable because he was wearing jeans and a button-up shirt, but the thought of Roxy not showing was driving him crazy. He paced back and forth.

"She'll be here. Are you kidding? After your awesome fight last night? You were incredible." Roger made his right hand into a fist and stuck it out in front of him. "'When the rhymes are over, it's lights out.' Wow, what a line."

Cedric looked around the restaurant at the few patrons. He didn't want to have to try to talk to Roxy with others in hearing range. "If she comes, where can we have some privacy?"

"Mi casa es su casa," Roger said. "The room in the back that is used for birthday parties is empty. Y'all can go back there. I'll make sure you're not bothered."

Cedric nodded then looked back out the window. Finally he saw Roxy's car. "Oh God, it's her." He looked down quickly to make sure he had nothing on his shirt even though he hadn't eaten all day. He ran his hand through his hair then opened the door for her as she approached.

Roxy entered the Frosty Freeze with a big smile. She wore loose jeans with holes in the knees. Real holes made over time, not the jeans manufactured that way. They matched her old faded t-shirt but were a stark contrast to her bright, new, pink sneakers. Her blond curls bounced up and down over her beautiful blue eyes as she walked. She wore no makeup nor needed to.

Cedric stood there in a trance as if wondering if the vision was real. He snapped out of it when he saw she wasn't alone.

"You came," Roxy said with a smile as she walked over to him and gave him a hug.

"Well, you know, I had nothing better to do anyway." Then he looked at her escort. "Good to see you again, Madison."

Madison nodded. "And you, Cedric."

Roxy giggled.

"Uh, Roger said we could use the back room." Cedric motioned with his hand and followed behind as Roxy walked toward the party area. But he stopped halfway across the room when he realized Madison was following too.

"Hey, Madison," Cedric said as he abruptly turned to face her, causing her to suddenly stop. "Do you like milkshakes?"

Madison's eyes rolled. "Oh, I love them?"

"Have you tried Roger's signature Peanut Butter Milkshake?"

Madison turned to look at Roger behind the counter. "No, I have not."

"It's incredible," Cedric said. "And he's going to

make one special just for you. Right, Roger?"

Roger grinned. "Absolutely."

"But here's the thing," Cedric said putting his hand on Madison's upper back and guiding her back toward Roger near the front entrance, "the taste is not even the best thing about the shake."

Madison looked confused. "What is?"

"It's the making of it," Cedric answered. "Wait until you see how it's made. It's like an illusion. It's magical. It's something you will never forget."

"Really?"

Cedric nodded and looked to Roger, which was his cue to take over.

"Oh yes," Roger said. "People come from all over to see this. Just take a seat here." He motioned for Madison to sit in front of the ice cream counter. "And I'll make you the most awesome shake in the world."

As Madison positioned herself on the stool, Cedric turned to catch up with Roxy who was waiting patiently for him. He looked back to see Roger holding a big jar of Peter Pan Peanut Butter, and the last thing he heard was: "And this is the secret magical elixir discovered by the ancient…"

After they entered the room, Cedric closed the door and pulled out a chair from the first table. Roxy took a seat and Cedric pulled out the chair beside her and sat there. His palms were sweating and he felt like the collar of his t-shirt under the button-up was cutting off his air supply. In fact, the entire room seemed to be stuffy as if the oxygen was being depleted.

"So," Cedric said swallowing hard, "what is this

mysterious meeting about?"

Roxy took a deep breath. "I don't know how to begin. I'm not even sure I have the courage to tell you. Uh… hey, you know what I remembered?" It was obvious she was stalling by changing the subject. "Back in the third grade when those two boys were picking on me and calling me names."

Cedric smiled. It was one of his fondest and most vivid memories, etched in intricate detail into his brain. "Yeah, vaguely. Seems I remember something along those lines."

Roxy continued. "I was so scared and was ready to burst into tears, but you walked over and punched both of them in the nose without even saying a word." She took a moment to laugh. "They never bothered me again. Every time after that, whenever I felt threatened, I'd come running to you and you would always protect me."

Cedric was enjoying this trip down memory lane. He never knew Roxy also remembered these events. "Well, I had to be your bodyguard. You paid me, remember?"

Roxy squinted. "Paid you? Oh that's right. I gave you my Little Debbie from my lunch one day."

Cedric nodded.

"Wow," Roxy said, "I never knew the value of those snacks. That one little brownie bought your protection forever."

"Well, you know, in prison it's cigarettes; in elementary it's sugar."

Roxy laughed. "And I thought it was because I

was pretty. Now I know it wasn't affection as much as confection."

Cedric laughed loudly. He loved Roxy's wit and sense of humor.

"But I was pretty then, wasn't I?" she asked.

'You were…" Cedric began with enthusiasm but quickly dialed it back a notch. "You were not the ugliest girl in our class."

"I remember how you would just sit and stare at any boy who dared speak to me."

"And I remember how you would want everyone to see every coloring page you created. You would have thought you were Picasso."

Roxy nodded. "I was the best artist in the class. I think I still am."

Cedric nodded in agreement. Roxy was indeed a wonderful artist.

"And I could talk to you about anything back in those days. And I always pretended to be a grownup. When you would get hurt, which was far too often, I'd pretend to put medicine or bandages on. Like when you punched those two kids in third grade, one of them must have had a bony nose because you had a little cut on your middle knuckle. I said in my best grownup voice, 'Let me see your hand'." She reached out her hand.

Cedric just stared.

"Come on, let me see your hand."

Cedric gladly placed his hand in hers.

"Oh my God," Roxy exclaimed when she saw the cuts and bruises. "I know this didn't come from that Ty guy." She looked into Cedric's eyes as if to scorn.

"You're not in the third grade anymore." Reaching into her purse, she pulled out some medicated wipes and proceeded to clean the injured areas. "So, are you going to tell me how this happened?"

"Playing with some grown men after the pep rally."

Roxy wiped hard as if to protest. "And how many did you play with?"

"About a dozen."

"A dozen?" Roxy gasped.

Cedric shrugged. "More or less."

"What am I going to do with you?" she asked. "Tell me all about it."

"No," Cedric replied. "It's time for you to tell me what you brought me here to tell me, if you've mustered the courage."

Roxy rolled up the little wipe and placed it on the table and took another deep breath. She stood and walked behind her chair. "I think I have. Well, you know I haven't had a lot of luck with boyfriends."

Cedric chuckled. He knew that it was no fault of hers, but rather that most boys in school were not mature enough for Roxy. She might have looked the classic cheerleader, but she was very intelligent and loved to read even more than Cedric did.

"I finally came to realize that it's what's in here that's important." She tapped her heart and then her head. Looking right into Cedric's eyes, she continued. "I think I have found that special someone, and I think I should let him know because I'm sure he feels the same about me."

Cedric's heart was racing. He sat there frozen not knowing what to say, a rare scenario for him indeed.

Roxy sat again and took both of Cedric's hands. "Wow. Your hands are so hot now."

Silence.

"Anyway," Roxy continued, "I think I'm in love. No, I'm certain of it."

Cedric could only nod.

"He's very smart and I'm certain he likes the same music, books, and movies I do. And he's a football player on our school team."

Cedric's breathing escalated. Could this really be happening? It was surreal.

"He's tall…"

"Yes," Cedric said.

"Strong…"

"Yes."

"Intelligent…"

"Yes."

"And slender."

Cedric's dream came crashing down. He pulled his hands away and sat up straight.

"What's wrong?" Roxy asked.

"Nothing," Cedric said. "My legs were starting to cramp. Please go on."

"That's all," Roxy said. "I think I'm in love with him. But I've only seen him a few times from a distance, three times over the summer, and then at last night's pep rally."

"Wait a minute. You've never even talked with him?" Cedric asked after finally regaining his composure.

Roxy shook her head.

"That's crazy," Cedric said throwing both arms up in the air on either side. "For all you know this guy is a buffoon. How many guys have you broken up with or not ever dated because they didn't match what you were looking for in intellect and wit? You have always held guys to a higher standard. Now you've fallen for a guy you know nothing about. He must be very handsome. I'm totally shocked at this."

Roxy smiled and shook her head. "No, it's not that. I mean yes, he is handsome, but that's not the attraction. Well, it helped a little. But others have told me all about him. And I can tell from looking at him. I can read his soul in his eyes."

"Our eyes do give us away," Cedric said while at the same time wondering why Roxy could not read his. "So he's on the football team? Who is it? What is his name?"

"Chris Nevil."

Cedric's brow lowered. "Nevil? I don't know that name. He's not a football player."

"Yes," Roxy said. "He just transferred from Western Hills."

Cedric knew the town and school, which about an hour from their own, but they were a different conference so they never played each other. He got up from his chair and walked a few feet away. "Well," he said, his back to Roxy and the tone in his voice conveying his disappointment, "we fall pretty fast, don't we?" Turning to look back at her, he added, "I don't understand the reason you're telling me all this."

"Because I know how you guys are with new players. I've heard the stories."

Cedric laughed. "All new players have to go through initiation. It's just good natured fun. Is that what you've heard?"

"Yes," Roxy said, "I think it's childish."

"I guess you're right, but boys will be boys."

Roxy shook her head. "Well, I thought maybe you could take it easy on Chris. All the guys look up to you and will do whatever you say."

Cedric couldn't believe what he was hearing. "Wait a minute. Am I getting this right? You're asking me to protect your little boyfriend, the boyfriend you're in love with yet have never met? And that's what you brought me here today to talk about?"

Roxy smiled and nodded. "I thought since you and I have always been such good friends, maybe you could be his friend too."

Cedric simply stared at Roxy for several seconds. "And that's what you ask of me?"

She nodded and took Cedric's hands in her own. "Yes."

Several more seconds passed until finally Cedric sighed. "Okay. I will look after your little guy and be his friend."

"And not let anyone pick on him?"

"No."

"Or let him get into any fights."

"No, never."

Roxy hugged Cedric. "You're the best friend anyone could have." She pulled back and took Cedric's hands in hers again.

Cedric stared into her eyes.

Suddenly Roxy became uncomfortable. "Well, I really must be going." She pulled away and walked to the door. As she opened the door, she turned back. "Please ask Chris to call me. I want to know all about him. Oh, you should call me too because you still have to tell me about your fight one day. A dozen grown men? That's so amazing. A dozen men. That must have taken a lot of courage."

Cedric watched as Roxy walked out of the party room and out the front door of the restaurant, Madison following close behind. He then closed the party room door and leaned against it, his head resting on his right forearm. "Not as much as coming here today," he whispered to himself. He wanted to go home. He wasn't sure how he felt. It wasn't quite anger, or depression, or confusion. Finally it dawned on him. He recognized the feeling although he had never felt it before. He felt defeated.

CHAPTER SIX

"How did it go?" Cap asked as Cedric walked toward the entrance of the Frosty Freeze.

Cedric lowered his eyes and kept walking. "I'm going home."

That told Cap all he needed to know. "But the whole team is coming. It's our regular get-together time. They'll be here any second. Of course I told them about last night and they're dying to hear you tell them about it."

Cedric clearly wasn't in the mood. He stopped and considered if he wanted to try to get out before everyone got there or ride out the storm.

"Maybe I can stop them," Cap said.

"Don't bother." Cedric turned and walked back into the middle of the room.

As Cedric finished that sentence, the front door opened and in walked the entire football team, cheering and laughing. They flowed around Cedric and Cap like lava. Several surrounded Cedric and patted him on the back. Cedric smiled and accepted the congratulatory gestures, though his heart was dying inside.

Most of the players took a seat and ordered something to eat. They took up over half of the seating.

Cap and Cedric sat at a table together.

Roger and his two sisters passed out menus.

"I see a lot of new faces," Cedric said looking over his teammates.

'Yes," Cap said in agreement as he too scanned the group. "I hope some of them can play. Someone has to pick up our slack."

Cedric laughed. "Indeed. This whole town has gone crazy with expectation. It would be nice to have someone else with whom to blame our failure."

Cap smiled but it vanished. He very much wanted to ask Cedric about the meeting with Roxy. He was sure he knew how it had gone, but wanted details and wondered what it was really about, though he dared not ask with so many others so close by. But he alone could see beyond Cedric's jubilant forced façade.

A little while later Roger and his sisters began bringing out everyone's orders. Then, much to Cedric's surprise, Roger tactfully slid a tray in front of him with a hamburger, fries, and fountain drink.

"Enjoy, everyone," Roger said and walked back to the counter before Cedric could protest.

Cedric smiled and ate, savoring every bite. He rarely got to eat away from his own home. His diet consisted mostly of junk food, because it was cheap and he and his mom never had much money to spend after bills were paid.

After they ate, Cap and Cedric walked over to the counter to talk with Roger. Cap grabbed Cedric by the arm and nodded toward the entrance. There stood Anthony Royal in the open doorway. This was not his regular hangout. His presence alone was enough to give everyone pause, especially after what Cedric did to his friend last night. It was very plausible that he was here for revenge.

"Cedric," Anthony said as he walked in and the door closed behind him, "I would like to express my admiration for your impressive performance last night. I hope you're well today after such a lively evening."

This made Cedric smile. "I am. Thank you. That is very kind of you."

Anthony nodded. "Of course. We might not be best friends, but it doesn't mean we can't be civil. After all, you are a unique individual: athlete and intellectual."

"Again, thank you."

Anthony nodded. "I understand that besides beating up innocent people, you are also a decent writer. Hard to believe, but I have heard that."

"You flatter me, sir."

"As you know," Anthony continued, oblivious to the sarcasm, "my father owns the newspaper. Would you care to join our team? We were thinking we could hire you as a columnist."

"That would be great," Cap said.

Cedric was skeptical. "Really?"

"Why not?" Anthony asked. "We could run two articles a week and pay you fifty dollars per article. Would that work out for you?"

"That sounds great," Cap said. "Cedric, you could work from home and you could certainly use the money."

"Why would you do that?" Cedric asked.

"I know we've had our differences," Anthony said, "but this is strictly a business arrangement. Just get us the articles a few days in advance to give us time to rewrite them so they conform to our readers."

Cedric laughed. "It wouldn't be my writing if you rewrite it."

"It's standard practice," Anthony said as he sat at an empty table. He looked around at all the faces looking back at him. Without looking back at Cedric, he continued. "Everything in the paper is edited before it goes to press."

"Thanks but no thanks," Cedric said.

Anthony turned to look at Cedric. "It could work into even more money down the road. Who knows, this could be the start of an exciting career for you. Isn't that the important thing?"

"No," Cedric said. "Not even close. My writing is a part of me. I could no more prostitute it out than I could my foot, my hand, or my soul."

"You are so stubborn," Anthony snapped.

Cedric smiled. "Again... thank you."

Just then another player came in carrying an old shoe. "Look what I found by the old saw mill. Cedric must have knocked this one out his shoes."

The group erupted in laughter.

"Who was behind it?" the player holding the shoe asked.

"Who cares?" Anthony asked with no remorse and no admission. He stood up quickly and again directed his words to Cedric. "You grab the bull, you get the horns."

Cedric walked over to his teammate and took the shoe from him and presented it to Anthony. "Can you please make sure your friend gets this back?"

Anthony's face turned red as he ignored the gesture. "Is this a Native American thing?"

"What do you mean?" Cedric asked.

"With some tribes, they believed the greater one's enemy, the greater it made them. Is that why you act this way? Is that why you insist on insulting those greater than you?"

"If that is true," Cedric answered, "then you being my enemy makes me almost nothing."

Anthony spun around and went out the door as everyone cheered. Well, not everyone.

"What is wrong with you?" Cap asked.

"What?"

"He was willing to forget and he was offering you a real job doing something you love." Cap shrugged and raised both arms beside him. "Was that so bad?"

"It was an insult," Cedric said. "And not even a subtle one. He doesn't want to be my friend or my employer."

"I'm not saying to make him your friend," Cap said, "but you don't have to make every powerful person an enemy."

"What's wrong with enemies? Didn't you just hear? They make a person great."

"There's no talking to you," Cap said.

"What do you want me to do, Cap?" Cedric's voice became elevated to the point of making all other conversations stop. "You want me to kiss his ass just to get my writings in the newspaper? No, thank you. Whose ass will be next? What price will I put on my dignity the next time? Shall I ignore the fine print and sign my name every time there's a chance to make a dollar? No, thank you. Shall I turn a blind eye and a deaf ear to every truth I hold sacred in the hopes that someone might recognize me as I walk down the street? No, thank you. Shall I sell off little bits and pieces of my soul until the day I wake up and no longer know who I am? No, thank you and again I thank you. But… to choose my own path, to write when and what I want, to fight when and who I want, that's the path of integrity that leads to manhood. I am who I am and if the world doesn't like it, they can form a long line starting right here to bend down and kiss my fat ass. I don't need anyone."

"That sounds great, Cedric," Cap said. "You don't need anyone. Shout it from the rooftops, but to me whisper the real reason. Whisper and tell me that Roxy doesn't love you."

Cedric looked at his friend, nodded, and patted him on the shoulder. "I need to be by myself for a while. I'll be back in a minute." He walked back to the party room and started to open the door.

"Wait," one of the players called out. "Cedric, tell us about your adventure after the pep rally."

"I will in a few minutes," Cedric said and disappeared into the back room, closing the door behind him.

"Dang it," the same player said. "I want to hear about it now."

"What's the rush?" another player at the table asked.

"It will be good for the newbies to hear," the first player said with a smile while motioning with his head toward a guy sitting at a table by himself. He nodded for the other two at his table and the three got up and went over and sat with the new player.

"Hey there," the first player said. "What's your name?"

"I'm Chris Nevil," Chris said and extended his hand.

The three players shook his hand.

"Welcome to Frenchtown, Chris," a second player offered. "We're excited to have you here."

"Thank you."

"Chris," the first player said, "we want to give you some advice, you being new here and all. It could save your life, so pay attention. There's only one subject that's taboo here in Frenchtown."

"Yeah, what's that?" Chris asked.

The third player twisted him around to face him and began to rub his belly.

"What?" Chris asked. "The stom—"

"Don't ever say that word," the first player said. "Don't ever say anything that might be mistaken to sound like it."

"You saw that fellow there," the second player said motioning to the party room. "He has already pulverized many fools who have accidentally referred to that subject."

"If you enjoy walking…" the first player said.

"Or talking…" the second player said.

"Or breathing…" the first player added.

"Then don't mention anything obtuse, circular, sphere-like, or orb-like." the second player said.

"If you do," the third player finally spoke, "kiss your ass goodbye, boy."

Chris's face turned red and he got up from the table as the three continued to laugh at him. He saw Cap and had already recognized him as being a team leader. He walked across the room and up to him. "Excuse me, sir. I'm new here so I don't know the proper protocol."

"What are you talking about?" Cap asked.

"Some of your boys are being jerks. What should I do?"

Cap shook his head. "You've got two choices: stand up for yourself or be picked on all year."

"Thank you." Chris nodded and walked away.

Cap tried to figure out what that was all about.

Chris walked past the table with the three obnoxious players and sat at another empty table by himself.

Cedric came out of the party room.

"All right," the first player said, "Let's hear it."

Everyone grew quiet as Cedric stood in the middle of them and began.

Cedric looked around at his anxious audience. "Well, boys, it was a fun night, I'll tell you that. What should I do? Should I slither away from responsibility and spit on our freedom of speech? I wouldn't be able to look myself in the mirror. But I knew I couldn't let anyone hurt one of our own. It was a dark night as we walked away from the school and I had a huge lump in my—"

"Stomach."

If someone had yelled "Fire!" it wouldn't have had as serious a response. The room grew deafeningly quiet as all eyes turned to seek out the source of the suicidal diatribe.

Cedric also sought out the culprit and saw him sitting at the table all alone. "Who... Is... That... Boy... There?" he said very slowly to no one in particular while pointing at the perpetrator.

"He's a new player," Cap answered.

Cedric smiled a wicked smile. "You don't say. Well isn't that great? It's initiation time, fellows." He stepped quickly toward the new guy and everyone knew what was coming. They had witnessed it many times.

Chris swallowed hard and stood to defend himself.

"His name is Chris Nevil," Cap added.

Cedric stopped in his tracks and stood staring for several seconds. His demons played tug-of-war with his mind. He wanted so much to continue. He wanted so much to find a release for the fire that had been ignited in the meeting with Roxy. But he had given his word, and given it to the girl he loved, had always loved. He knew deep down he had to control his anger this one time. "Fine," he said, and stood there staring at Chris while breathing so hard the guys near him could hear it. Then, much to everyone's amazement, he turned and very slowly walked back to his spot and continued the story.

The tension still filled the room, but was now mixed with confusion. No one knew why Cedric had not proceeded to beat the crap out of this person. After all, he had never turned the other cheek — ever.

Cedric gave one more look to his new nemesis, his new teammate, and as Roxy would have it, his new friend. He growled under his breath and began again. "Anyway, like I was saying, I had a lump in my *throat*. I wasn't sure if the danger was real, but I had a feeling—"

"In your gut," Chris said.

"In my *heart*!" Cedric loudly corrected and took a few steps toward Chris again.

Chris stood again, but again it was premature.

Cedric spun around quickly and again returned to his spot and continued. "Suddenly a man charged and I gave him a vicious—"

"Belly butt."

"*Head butt*!" Cedric's voice got louder. "He fell flat on his—"

"Tummy."

"*Back*! Suddenly they were all around me. One threw a punch but I blocked it with my—"

"Midsection."

"*Arm*! I blocked it with my arm. One got in a stinging—"

"Belly rub." Chris was now enjoying himself.

"*Jab*! I decided to hit them with all my—"

"Fat!" Chris almost yelled.

"That's it." Cedric had had enough, looking and pointing at Chris. "Let's me and you step out back."

Chris bravely followed Cedric out the back door of the restaurant. As much as they all wanted to, the others knew not to follow. In the back area there was a little graveled road for deliveries, a large green dumpster, and an old wooden bench, but no cars and no other people were present. As Cedric approached Chris he quickly threw up his fists in a boxing configuration.

Cedric paused a few feet from him and placed a hand on each hip. He stood there like a superhero might sum up the villain. All that was missing was a cape. He looked Chris over from head to toe. "Well, you got a pair on you; I'll give you that. That's a good thing at least."

Chris kept his fists up. "What does that mean?"

Cedric sat on the bench. "It means I wouldn't want Roxy dating a coward."

Chris's eyes lit up. "You know Roxy?"

"We're best friends."

"Best friends? You and her?"

Cedric shrugged. "Well, very old friends at least."

"I didn't know," Chris said. "I have very much been wanting to meet you. Everyone tells me what a great football player you are. I am so impressed."

"Yes," Cedric said, "you sure seem so with all those fat remarks."

Chris blushed. "I am so sorry about that." Chris sat beside Cedric. "You think she likes me?"

"I do. She has told me as much."

"Wow," Chris said. "I can't believe it. She is so beautiful."

"She is that and so much more."

"What do I do?" Chris asked.

"Let me give you her number," Cedric said, "so you can call her."

Chris looked as if he had seen a monster. "Oh no, I can't."

"What do you mean?"

"I just can't," Chris said. "Once I call her, it's over. I'm not smooth at all. I start stammering like an idiot and my mind goes blank."

"You did not sound like an idiot when you attacked me just now."

"Yeah, but you're a guy," Chris said. "Besides, it's easy to pick a fight. No, I'm never at a loss for words around the fellows, but when I try to talk to a girl, my brain shuts down and I become a zombie. I'm just one of those helpless morons who can't say the right things to girls."

Cedric looked up toward the sky. "I always thought I would be pretty good at that, if ever given the chance."

"If I was clever like you," Chris said.

Cedric smiled. "If I were slim like you. Together we could put Casanova to shame."

"Maybe we could trade brains for a while," Chris joked.

A light went off above Cedric's head. "That's not a bad idea."

"What?"

Cedric smiled and stood up. "Use my brain. Let me be your secret weapon, your voice from the shadows to woo the maiden. We'll practice conversations before you call her and I can write letters for you. We'll give her the best version of you of which we can collaborate."

Chris stood also. He smiled and then frowned. "I don't know. It sounds dishonest. What if she catches on?"

"Come on. Isn't she worth it? Let's do it," Cedric almost yelled as he grabbed Chris by each arm.

"Why does this mean so much to you?"

Cedric calmed down and let go of Chris's arms. "It doesn't. I mean, it will be fun and interesting like a science experiment. Wouldn't it be tragic if your disability kept you two apart? Don't you think she's worth it?"

The idea began to make sense in Chris's mind. "You're right. She is worth it. Let's do this, my friend."

Cedric put his hand on Chris's shoulder. "My friend."

CHAPTER SEVEN

Mrs. Nevil opened the front door and stared at the presence of the large individual blocking out the entire scenery beyond him. Unsure what to do, she simply stood there for several seconds waiting for the moment to make sense. Finally she found her voice. "Can I help you?"

Cedric nodded. "I'm here for your first-born child."

"What?" Mrs. Nevil stepped back a pace. "Oh wait. Are you Cedric?"

"Yes ma'am. I'm sorry."

She bent over laughing and slapped her thigh. "Come on in, Cedric. You had me going for a spell. Chris, your friend Cedric is here."

Chris came out of his bedroom. "Hey, come on back."

Cedric nodded to Chris's mom and walked toward the back. As he walked through the kitchen, he saw Chris's father sitting at the table reading the *Gazette*.

"Dad, this is Cedric," Chris said.

His dad looked up. "Nice to meet you, Cedric."

"You too, sir."

Mr. Nevil glanced back at the paper. "Says here

you boys could go all the way this year. What do you say?"

"To be honest, sir, I kind of wish people would stop talking about it."

"I can understand that," Mr. Nevil said. "I imagine that puts way too much pressure on you boys. People should be more considerate, but you know that isn't going to happen."

Cedric nodded. He understood human nature better than just about anyone. "That's true, sir."

"Are you going to stay for dinner?" Mrs. Nevil asked.

Cedric inhaled the wonderful aroma. "If you twist my arm, I will."

Chris's father made a shocked face. "I'm not touching those arms."

Everyone laughed.

"Come on," Chris said and turned to walk back to his room.

"And thanks, Cedric," Mrs. Nevil added, "for helping Chris with his homework."

Cedric looked at Chris, whose expression was one of getting caught in a lie, and laughed inside at the trouble he could cause at the moment. He could easily conjure up a shocked expression and say something like, "Homework? I'm just here to help him get a date." But of course he decided not to. What he did say was this: "It's my pleasure, ma'am. He just doesn't appear to be catching on in most of his classes. It's almost as if his mind was someplace else."

"His mind has always wandered," his dad said.

"Takes after his mother."

His mom smiled and was either embarrassed or proud of that assessment.

Cedric grinned and followed Chris back to his room.

Chris sat on his bed.

Cedric sat on the bed also, but the soft mattress sank too low. "Well, this is not going to work."

"Hold on," Chris said, got up, and left the room. He returned with a wooden chair from the dining table. That worked much better for Cedric.

Cedric scanned the bedroom. The room was beautifully painted and shelves adorned all four walls. All the rooms he had seen so far were neat and decorated with semi-expensive furniture and décor and the house itself was a large brick home. On the shelves of Chris's bedroom were trophies and awards. Cedric got up and looked at all of them: baseball, football, and even one tennis trophy. He concentrated on the contents of one shelf. "You were an Eagle Scout?"

"I was."

Cedric smiled. "So you always help little old ladies across the street?"

"Of course," Chris said. "Wouldn't you?"

Cedric shook his head. "I might throw them across." He retook his seat.

"So," Chris said, "what's the best way to get a girl like Roxy to fall for you?"

"We start with this letter," Cedric said and pulled the folded sheet of paper from his pocket. "You just need to sign it and have someone pass it to her in school."

Chris opened the letter and read.

"My dearest Roxy,

In my seventeen years I have beheld wonders beyond description. I have witnessed miracles of faith, chance, and even happenstance. I have seen the face of God in sunrises, sunsets, waterfalls, and all of nature. But all of it pales in comparison to the first time I looked into your eyes, past the natural beauty that Mother Nature has kindly heaped upon your tender complexion as I peered through the gateway to your soul and was awestruck. Only in that briefest of moments did the universe make sense to me. Only then did I understand the meaning of creation, of life, and of love. Only then did I have a glimpse of my own destiny and my own purpose. Only then did I know what path I would choose above all others. To make you think and dream would be like winning a Pulitzer. To make you smile or laugh would be like winning a Nobel Prize. And dare I pretend to one day surpass all those lofty goals and make you the one thing I myself can only dream about – to make you mine."

Cedric waited patiently as Chris read the letter a second time.

"Oh my goodness," Chris said, "This is incredible. How do you write like this?"

"They're just words," Cedric answered. "They're normal words even. I didn't create any of them; I just put them in a certain order."

"But I could never do this. I can't use words like this."

"You better learn," Cedric said. "Consider some of the greatest literature in history. What do you think is the best book ever written?"

"The Bible?"

Cedric chuckled. "Okay, granted, it's hard to top that one. But maybe something not quite two thousand years old. Think fiction."

Chris looked like he was in pain as he tried to think.

"Never mind," Cedric said. "I'll pick one. Let's say *A Tale of Two Cities.*"

"Okay. I haven't read it."

Cedric smirked. "I'm painfully aware of that. But some people who do read consider it to be one of the best stories ever. Do you know how it begins?"

Chris shook his head.

"It was the best of times, it was the worst of times, it was the age of wisdom, it was the age of foolishness."

"It was both?" Chris asked.

"You're killing me. That's not the point. The point

is: have you ever heard those individual words before?"

Chris nodded. "Sure. They're simple words."

"Exactly. See, Charles Dickens did not have to make up words to write a classic story. He used the same words you and I use."

"Oh, okay."

Cedric smiled. "Now you're catching on. You see, with a girl like Roxy, you can't just say, 'Hey baby, you're hot.' She would be insulted. Some girls might not be, but she would."

"So I have to learn to use words I already know but in the right way."

Cedric gave him a thumb up. "There you go. Imagine if you were on safari and your survival depended on how to use a very specific hunting rifle. You'd learn to use it, wouldn't you?"

"I'm not a big hunter," Chris said.

Cedric's large face turned red. "It's a metaphor, moron."

"Oh, okay. Yes, I'd learn how to use the gun."

"Well, now you face your greatest prey, far more dangerous than any jungle creature, far more elusive than any exotic bird, and far more valuable than all of them combined. And you have one weapon — words."

Chris took a deep breath and nodded. "So what's the plan?"

"We start with this letter. Luckily Roxy loves the written word, so writing to her will delight her even more than calling. When the time is right we shall graduate to the phone and I will have conversational notes for you to follow, notes that will impress upon her that you are a man of vision and character who can converse on a multitude of subjects."

Chris stared at Cedric as if he had just given a fast description of how to work a complex Calculus problem.

Cedric noticed. "Don't worry. One step at a time. Now, let's start with your school demeanor."

"What do you mean?"

"Well," Cedric said, "that might be the only place she sees you for a while and her image of you must never be imbrued."

"Be what?"

"Tainted. She must always see you as calm and in control. No girl likes a man who can't control his temper or gets upset every time someone picks on him or tries to get him riled."

Chris smiled. "But you do."

"You're cruising," Cedric replied. "Don't think I won't slap you around just because your parents are in the next room."

"Okay," Chris said still smiling at his own humorous remark. "What do I do if I see her in the halls? Do I ignore her?"

"Idiot. There's not a human on this planet who likes being ignored. Just look her in the eyes and smile, but keep walking at the same pace. Come, let's take a walk and talk some more."

The duo left the bedroom and walked through the kitchen.

"Dinner is almost ready," Mrs. Nevil said.

Cedric stopped. "I wouldn't want to be rude.

We'll take a walk after we eat."

Chris retrieved the chair from the bedroom so all four could sit around the table as his mother began to set pots and pans filled with culinary wonders onto the table on potholders.

His father folded up the newspaper and laid it on the antique sideboard behind him. "Glad you could join us this evening, Cedric. Chris has told us a lot about you. He says you're the smartest one in the class and will most likely be the valedictorian?"

Cedric shrugged. "Well, it's not a very impressive bunch."

"Oh, I doubt that," his father replied. "I understand you have also won math trophies."

Cedric nodded.

"I was horrible at math," Mrs. Nevil said. "I hated it."

Cedric smiled. "I think you're in the majority there, ma'am."

That seemed to make her feel better. "Do you plan to go to college on an academic scholarship?" she asked.

"I'm not sure," Cedric answered honestly. "It would be nice to receive a football scholarship."

"That would be very nice," Chris's mom said.

Chris and his father nodded in agreement.

Cedric couldn't believe what he was seeing on the table: pork chops, mashed potatoes, macaroni & cheese, green beans, salad, and toasted French bread.

"Sweet tea, Cedric?" Mrs. Nevil asked.

"Yes, ma'am."

Mr. Nevil said a prayer as Chris and his mom bowed their heads.

Cedric was still in awe of the food.

"Let's eat," Mr. Nevil said.

Cedric needed no further invitation. He put some of everything in his plate. Everything had so much flavor. But as amazed as he was at the food, it was what happened next that really stunned him.

"How was your day, son?" Mr. Nevil asked looking at Chris while chewing on a piece of meat.

"Good, Dad."

"When does football practice begin?" his father asked.

"Next week."

"You going to look after our boy?" his mother asked. "Will you, Cedric?"

"I have to," Cedric answered. Then he noticed the confused look on Chris and his parents' faces. "Uh, I mean we always try to take care of the new guys."

"That's nice," Mrs. Nevil said.

"Well, we'll be there to cheer you guys on," his father said. "We have been to every one of Chris's games. What position do you play, Cedric?"

"Offensive tackle."

Mr. Nevil nodded. "Very tough position. You boys just go out there this season and have fun. Everything will fall in place like it's supposed to."

"What does your mom and dad do?" Mrs. Nevil asked.

Cedric stopped eating, holding a fork of mac & cheese midair. The football talk was fun. This, not so much. "My dad left when I was a baby and my mom is disabled."

"Oh I'm sorry," she said.

And that subject was never brought up again.

The rest of the meal went the same. Pleasant conversation complemented the fine cooking. Cedric found himself enjoying the company rather a lot.

After dinner Cedric and Chris took a walk around the neighborhood.

"My family's pretty strange, huh?"

"Oh yes," Cedric said. "Beautiful house, terrific food, and delightful conversation. Seriously, Chris, I never knew you had it so rough."

Chris nodded as if Cedric was serious.

"So let me ask you," Cedric said, "how many of the classics have you read?"

"Books?"

"Yes, doofus, books."

"Just the ones that were assigned reading in school," Chris answered.

Cedric rolled his eyes. "So basically only the books you were forced to read."

"Yeah. Is that bad?"

"Oh yes," Cedric said. "See, Roxy loves to read. She loves great literature because it's laced with incredible metaphors and similes. That's what stirs her soul. That's how to win her heart."

"So she wants someone to talk like that all the time?"

"You're hopeless," Cedric snapped. "No, not all the time. But we're talking about courting. When you court a girl, you pay attention to what she likes and try to use that to impress her. If you knew a girl loved Harley Davidsons, would you show up for a date riding a Yamaha Moped?"

Chris thought for a few seconds. "Does Yamaha even make a moped?" He laughed then quickly added. "I'm messing with you."

Cedric laughed. "That was a good one. I was about to clobber you. What if you knew a girl loved muscular biceps. What would you do?"

"That's more like it. I'd hit the gym harder."

"Exactly," Cedric said. "You wouldn't carry a set of dumbbells with you when you guys went to the movies or out to eat. But you would prepare to impress her by pumping iron so hopefully you can get to that stage. Does that make sense?"

"Yes, makes perfect sense. So you're my trainer and I'm pumping words to impress the girl?"

"Very well put, my friend."

Chris impressed himself. "So how do I learn to talk and write like this?"

"Practice," Cedric answered. "Let's pick an object and try an exercise." He stopped walking. "Look at this huge tree. How would you describe it?"

Chris stopped too and stared at the tree. "Uh… it's huge."

Cedric looked at him in disbelief.

"Okay, okay," Chris said and concentrated harder. "It's… uh… tall?"

"You're killing me."

"I don't know what to say," Chris said. "If it's so

easy, you do it."

Cedric looked at the tree and then closed his eyes. "An ancient wooden lifeform digs deep and grips the Earth with one hand while its other tries desperately to reach the stars in an effort to shade us with its timeless beauty."

"Holy crap," Chris said. "Yeah, that sounds a little better than 'tall'. How do you do that?"

"You can do it too. Now let's tackle a deeper subject. How would you describe your feelings for Roxy?"

"I like her."

Cedric took a deep breath. "You know you're going to get beaten before this night is over, don't you?"

Chris nodded. "I know."

"Then tell me how you feel."

Chris thought hard. "I can't even think straight when I see her. I get tongue-tied."

"Okay," Cedric said. "Not bad. Let's see if we can build on that. Whenever I see you, my mind divides itself, and all the parts that make us human: logic, hope, fear, desire, all rush away from my thoughts leaving me speechless."

"Wow," Chris said. "Will *you* go out with me? Seriously, you should be able to get any girl in school."

Cedric ignored the remark wondering how anyone as smart as Chris could even think such a thing. "Let's keep working."

The duo walked and worked on speaking for another two hours. Chris was starting to get the hang of it.

"I think we should call it a night," Cedric said. "You're doing much better."

"Thanks. You want to come back to the house? I can give you a ride home."

Cedric shook his head. "No, I'm not too far from here." He pointed the way they were walking.

"Okay," Chris said. "I'll see you in school tomorrow." He turned and walked back the way they had come.

Cedric watched until Chris faded into the darkness before he continued walking. But he wasn't quite ready to go home. He knew the area well where he now tread, and followed a familiar route. It was almost by habit or more like a scientific magnetic pull that affected him.

He came to a section in the road where there were no houses on one side, just empty overgrown lots. He stood beside a small tree and stared at the house across the street. It was a small two-story house, but neat, with yellow siding and white trim. The covered front porch played host to a wooden bench suspended by chains, which swung gently in the breeze. Several potted plants adorned the eve of the roof above the porch, the plants now drooping with the fall weather.

Two concrete benches graced the well-manicured lawn on each side of the concrete walkway that led from the curb to the steps. The house was built in the 1950s, as probably was the walkway because it had its share of cracks and chips.

The lights were on downstairs but not upstairs. Colorful illuminations flashed on the front curtains from a television set.

Cedric stared. He had been in this exact spot many times before. It was the house of Roxy's parents.

He looked longingly at the entire property. He had seen it many times in passing, and even more in his dreams.

"Please forgive me, my love," he whispered. "For a decade of agony, I have struggled to tell you how I feel. For a decade, I have failed miserably. I am a coward, but even cowards have the needs and desires of all mortal men. I have to be able to tell you what is in my heart, even if it comes to you from the lips of another."

The lights on the main floor went off and the upstairs curtains suddenly glowed.

"Sleep well, princess." He turned and walked away.

CHAPTER EIGHT

———— ❖ ————

"Good catch, Nevil," the coach said and patted Chris on the back as he returned to the offensive squad. Chris had proven he could run and catch well and the coach had already recognized him as a solid asset.

"Good catch, lover boy," Cedric said as they circled around into the huddle.

The other players laughed.

Chris laughed too. "Like an elk across the plains of Africa, leaping, grasping at the leather prize to make it one with me."

This time only Cedric laughed as the other players looked on in silence. Only he knew Chris was following his directions of learning to use similes and metaphors to describe everyday events.

"I don't know what that was," Cap said, "but I hope that was all of it."

Everyone laughed again.

"Wait, are elk in Africa?" Another player asked. "I'm thinking Canada."

"What's in Africa?" another asked.

The quarterback chimed in. "Gazelle."

Everyone agreed.

"But is 'leather' correct?" yet another asked. "Isn't

it called a pig skin?"

Cedric patted him on the helmet. "I'll explain that one later."

Stop the chatter," the coach commanded. "Let's run it again."

Practice went on. By the time it was over Cedric had consumed at least fifteen small cups of sports drink and not a dry spot could be found on his practice jersey. Even though it was neither a full dress nor full contact practice, and the fall weather was pleasantly cool, just the exertion was enough to make Cedric perspire profusely.

But it was paying off for the Cavaliers as they had won their first four games, and won them easily.

After practice the players all showered, dressed back in their school clothes, and headed home. Chris gave Cedric a ride as always.

"Roxy asked me to call her Saturday afternoon," Chris said.

"I know; I read the letter."

"What should I do?"

Cedric was not going to be able to help Chris that day. He had a math tournament to go to in Murfreesboro. "I don't think you're ready to go solo," Cedric said. "Send her a note tomorrow in school with some excuse why you cannot."

"I don't want to be dishonest."

Cedric stared at Chris like he was nuts. "Dishonest?"

Chris shrugged his shoulders. "I know we're being dishonest every day, which is why I would like to avoid it whenever else possible."

"Wow. You really were an Eagle Scout. It's up to you, but I would suggest waiting until I can be there."

Chris didn't reply and Cedric knew what that meant.

"But I do have a letter I want you to look at," Chris said. "I mean I don't think I'm ready yet to write her on my own, but I want your opinion to see if I'm getting better."

Cedric was impressed with the initiative. "Do you have it with you?"

Chris pulled the folded letter out of his pocket and passed it to Cedric. "Please don't be mean?"

"Am I ever mean? You know what, don't answer that." Cedric opened the letter and read.

"My dearest Roxy,

Oh, how my world has grown since you came into it. Like the newborn baby who became Hercules, bursting at the seams with strength he never knew he had. My powers of perception have magnified a hundred fold. The air is different. The sky has come alive. The grass is greener than I ever re-membered. Everything in my world has expanded beyond the boundaries of their normal existence. But what has grown the most is my heart. Never did I know how much love it could hold. It's as if the world has grown ten

```
times it's size and here I sit on top
of it. And it's all because of you."
```

Cedric folded the paper and handed it back to Chris.

"Well," Chris asked. "What did you think? And you can be honest."

"Have you ever known me to be anything else?"

Chris laughed. "Sadly, no."

"Then I shall not deceive you now. I think it is a great letter."

Chris breathed a sigh of relief.

"I would only point out two things."

"And those are?" Chris asked.

"First," Cedric said, "the word 'its' has no apostrophe unless it means 'it is.' When you write 'its size,' leave that off. Secondly, repetitive words can weaken the writing."

Chris thought about the letter in his mind. "Which word?"

"The word 'world' is written three times in that short letter," Cedric said.

"Oh shoot," Chris said. "You're right."

"But other than that, it's very good. In fact, make those two small changes and I say it's good enough to send."

Chris smiled.

So did Cedric. "You are really starting to develop a way with words."

"Thanks to you," Chris said. "I appreciate everything you've done for me. I'm still not sure why you are helping me."

"Well, blame it on that old gypsy woman."

"What?"

Cedric looked over at Chris. "I didn't tell you about that?"

Chris shook his head.

"Oh my," Cedric began. "Right before I met you there was this woman who set up in a raggedy old tent right in the park in the middle of the square. Apparently she had gotten a permit from the city and was telling people's fortunes, you know with Tarot Cards and a crystal ball and everything. She looked to be over a hundred years old. Her gray hair came down to her waist and had a thousand beads. She couldn't have been over four feet and five inches."

Chris was mystified.

"Yes," Cedric continued. "And she had a patch over one eye. It was crazy. Her hand-written sign said she charged five dollars to look into your future. I happen to have that amount on me that day and walked into the tent and gave it to her.

"She had me sit across from her at this old table and began flipping cards over from the deck. Soon she had two matching cards and stared at me with her one good eye, which was a weird color of purple.

"Then she spoke. Her English was thick with like a Romanian accent and kind of hard to understand. 'Your destiny hangs in the balance,' she said. 'Your very soul is in danger of damnation unless you change your evil ways. Your opportunity approaches. A young man with a good heart will need your help. It's your choice to help him or not. But your decision will determine your fate.'

"'Who is it?' I asked. 'How will I know him?'

"'Easy,' she said. 'He will be the biggest most gullible idiot you ever met.'"

Chris laughed so hard he almost swerved off the road. "Oh my God. You had me going. I should have known you were pulling my leg."

Cedric nodded. "Yes, you should have known. It should have given it away when I said I had five dollars."

"Good point. Great story, though." Chris pulled up and let Cedric off in front of his house. "Good luck Saturday."

Cedric bent down and looked in through the passenger window. "You too, Chris. You too."

***

Miss Andrews wrung her hands like she always did when she was nervous. "All right, guys, this is it. We're about to take the written test. Remember, there is a penalty for guessing, so only answer the ones you know for sure."

It was the same spiel she gave the twelve members of the math team at every tournament. Four members made up the Geometry team, four for the Algebra II team, and four for the team Cedric and Roger was on, the Calculus team. And she was right. Wrong answers were graded with a negative mark, and some people, when it was all over, ended up with a negative score.

"Cedric?"

"Cedric?"

"Oh, sorry," Cedric said and looked at Miss Andrews.

"Where are you?" she asked. "Your mind is a million miles away. I need you focused."

Cedric nodded. "I'm sorry." But he couldn't stop worrying about Chris and Roxy. Chris had never spoken to her on the phone without Cedric being there to guide him and he had a very bad feeling about it. He had written plenty of notes to guide Chris, but even he couldn't think of everything.

Students from the same schools were separated and put into rooms with dozens of students from other schools. The test papers were handed out and the time clock was activated.

Cedric looked at the first problem but his thoughts betrayed him as he couldn't stop thinking about Chris calling Roxy. He shook his head as if that might sling the images from his mind. He concentrated on the first problem and realized it was something he knew well. He worked it out on scrap paper and wrote the answer in the box.

He continued on. About a third of the problems he knew how to do from working many similar equations. Many, however, consisted of math he had never even seen. But an amazing thing happened. As he stared at the unfamiliar problems, they began to become clear. Never having seen the formulas for these problems, he started coming up with his own.

He looked around the room in amazement. He had experienced moments on the football field where everything clicked and he was stronger, faster, and more alert. He could do no wrong and could even anticipate his opponent's strategies. But this was the first time that phenomenon had ever manifested itself in an academic pursuit.

As he contemplated the reason for it, he began to realize something else, something even more surprising. He was happy. He hadn't recognized the foreign emotion. But ever since he began helping Chris, it was as if a weight had been lifted from his shoulders. Maybe it was finally being able to say and write all the things to Roxy that he had always wanted to.

He smiled and threw himself into the math exam. When he was finished there were still ten minutes left on the clock and he had answered all forty questions and four tiebreakers.

All the students met up with their teammates in the halls afterward.

As was custom, Miss Andrews began questioning each student as to their performance and how they felt they did. She asked one particular question after each written portion of the tournaments: "How many did you answer?"

Answers ranged from eight to twelve.

"How many did you answer, Roger?"

Roger smiled. "I answered ten, but I think I got them all correct. Some of them were very tough."

She smiled and moved on.

Cedric was dreading the question.

"How do you think you did, Cedric?"

Cedric nodded. "I think I did very well, Miss Andrews."

"Great. How many did you answer?"

Cedric swallowed hard as he looked her in the eye and prepared for what he knew was inevitable. "I answered all of them."

There was no mistaking the disappointment in her expression. "How could you? You know you can't do that."

"I still think I did well," Cedric offered.

A few moments later an official brought the three pages, one for each division, and pinned them to the corkboard on the wall in the hall.

Cedric walked over quickly and located the Calculus division. As was the norm, only the top twenty high scores were posted. To make that list was deemed very impressive considering there were several hundred competitors. Cedric had never failed to make the cut, usually placing around the tenth highest score. But as he perused the names, he didn't see his… until he looked at the top. He was number one. His score was much higher than the person in second place.

He couldn't help but grin. He was on top of the world. Nothing could faze him.

"Hey, Gigantor, we can't see around you."

Roger gasped out loud.

Cedric's face turned red and he spun around to find the source of this insult. There stood a scrawny boy about five-feet-two with unbelievably thick eyeglasses. Cedric grabbed him around the neck with his mighty claw-like grip and pushed the kid's face right into the board. The boy's glasses tilted and almost fell off his face as his nose squashed into the cork material.

Cedric leaned in close. "Can you see the board now?"

"Yes, sir."

"What are you doing?" Miss Andrews snapped. "Let him go."

Cedric pulled the boy back and smiled as he straightened the boy's glasses and shirt. "Just helping my friend here get a good look at the results."

Miss Andrews shook her head.

At the awards ceremony, Cedric took first place and he walked to the stage to accept his trophy. His score was so high it made his team win first place also.

Miss Andrews was quite happy to be taking home two more first place trophies.

They drove back to the Frosty Freeze where they all had met early that morning, and Roger gave Cedric a ride home.

"Congratulations again, Cedric. This is one of the best days of my life."

Cedric nodded. "Me, too, my friend. Me, too."

It was after 8 p.m. when Cedric got home. He waved goodbye to Roger and started toward the front door. Since he and his mother had no telephone, he wanted to go to Chris's to find out how the phone call had gone without him, but he had been away all day and needed to check on his mother. He walked in and put his trophy in the front room closet. The room was almost dark. Just the illumination from the television softly cast light upon the almost bare living room.

His mom was sitting watching her favorite shows, which was about all she ever did. She was a small woman with grey hair that grew down her back and rarely saw a brush. Her wardrobe consisted of a red plaid button-up shirt and thin yellow pants. She smiled as he walked in but said nothing, simply returned her attention to the TV.

Cedric went into the kitchen and looked around. He could tell she hadn't eaten all day. He took a pack of wieners from the fridge and put them in a pot of water. Placing the pot on the stove and turning on the electric eye, he then took a small onion and cut it into tiny cubes.

When the wieners were cooked, he made a hotdog out of a slice of regular loaf bread with a little ketchup only. He took it on a paper plate along with a plastic cup filled with ice cubes and water into the living room and presented it to his mom.

She smiled again, took the plate, and instinctively slid the end of the hotdog into her mouth.

Cedric placed the cup of water on the little end table beside her chair then went back in the kitchen. He was starving. Miss Andrews had stopped at a convenience store on the way to Murfreesboro and everyone else had bought snacks and drinks, but not Cedric. He had no money as usual. There were seven other hotdogs in the pot, so Cedric got out seven pieces of bread and stacked them up on another paper plate. One-by-one he placed a cooked wiener on a slice of bread, smothered it in mustard and onions, and demolished it. He drank straight from a two-liter Diet Coke that he had taken out of the refrigerator also.

When he was finished, he went back to the living room and collected his mother's empty plate and plastic cup still half filled with water.

"I'm going to take a walk," he said as he kissed his mother on the forehead.

She looked up and nodded.

Cedric walked away from his house with plans to go to Chris's house and find out if he had in fact called Roxy and if it had gone well. But as he walked toward Chris's house, something caught his eye. There were lights filling the night sky behind the high school. He knew that was a large cleared area there that the town often used for special events, like concerts and even a small carnival that came through once a year. Curiosity got the better of him and he walked that way instead.

As he neared the area, he was surprised to see a circus had come to town. Colorful trucks and trailers adorned the perimeter of the grassy area. Circus workers were busy running electrical lines and trying to set up the main tent. Cedric strolled right through the middle of the calamitous scene as if he belonged there. No one paid him any mind.

Two men were trying to stand up a high metal pole as he walked past. They struggled but could not get it to stand up. Both men were small and short. Cedric reached up over them and shoved the pole and it stood straight up into place.

"Thanks," they both called out as Cedric waved and walked on.

Cedric saw something that really caught his attention: the trailers with the animals. He walked past cages with lions, bears, and various other circus animals. Then he saw something that made him smile. A few trailers down something long and gray was sticking out between the bars of yet another large cage. He walked closer.

Once he was in front of the trailer, he saw them: two large elephants. The female had her trunk outstretched and when Cedric walked up closer, she caressed his face with the tip of her trunk. The big male walked over and stuck his trunk through the bars and did the same.

Cedric chuckled and rubbed both trunks with his hands. "No guys, I'm not one of you. It's an easy mistake."

"They sure like you."

Cedric turned to see one of the men whom he had helped a little earlier with the metal pole. He smiled and looked back at his two new extremely large friends and whispered, "You're such a nice guy to make the circus elephants feel at home."

CHAPTER NINE

The next morning after the math tournament brought about a familiar scene: a large silhouette on the early morning sky moving slowing along a residential street toward the high school. The pink and yellow hues floating above the horizon announced the coming of the sun.

Cedric walked in slow motion. He loved going to the gym early on Sunday mornings because it was usually empty and he could work out alone. He carried only a towel to use for wiping sweat from his forehead. He never showered at the gym; just waited until he got home. He did not feel comfortable showering where other people might see him. He did it around the football players, but he still wasn't comfortable.

He arrived at the school gym and punched in the code to enter. It was free to use for students and faculty. He went in and walked to the area where an Olympic curl bar lay on a rubber mat in front of a mirror.

He shook his huge arms to get loose, stretched his neck side-to-side, and slid a forty-five-pound plate on each side of the bar. He squatted down and hoisted it up. As he curled the bar up to his chest with ease, he stared at his reflection in the mirror.

Cedric had no mirrors in his home or any use

for them. Even the medicine cabinet in the one bath-room had lost its mirror long ago. But the gym had mir-rors all along the two long walls. He stared at himself. That alone was enough to make him cringe, especially his huge waistline. He looked up at his round face. He had his mother's cheeks and eyes. But as he stared deep-er, past the surface, he saw someone else, someone he hadn't seen in a very long time and it made him sick to his stomach. He still harbored hateful feelings for this person, and he hoped he never saw him again. If he ever did, there was no telling what he might do. The few memories he still stored in the darkest recesses of his mind continued to haunt him. He kept these memories and feelings buried deep, but sometimes they crept to the surface.

> *"Stop feeding him. Put him to bed."*
> *"Let him cry. He can't still be hungry."*
> *"Look what you're doing. Nobody wants a fat son."*

Cedric curled faster, his teeth grinding. He set the weights down and added another forty-five pound plate on each side. That brought the total weight to just under two hundred pounds. He lifted it with effort and began the curling routine again. But his demons were not fin-ished with their teasing. He had a flashback to his first day of first grade.

> *"Hey fatty. You're a slob."*
> *"Look how fat he is."*
> *"Run, he's a monster and he's gonna eat you."*

The veins were bulging in Cedric's neck and beside his eyes. He curled the weight with pure hatred rushing through his veins. Faster. Faster.

"Hey, Cedric."

Cedric dropped the bar and it bounced off the rubber mat. He looked around and saw that Chris had come in the door. He steadied his breathing and grabbed his towel to wipe the sweat running down his face. His shirt already had a wet stain the size of a basketball.

"Hey. What are you doing here?

"I thought you would be here," Chris said. "How did the math thing go?

"*Math thing?*" Cedric asked. "Wow. Good thing I'm not helping you learn to use words."

Chris laughed. "You know what I mean."

Cedric sat on a flat padded bench still breathing heavily. "It went well. I took first place."

"That's awesome."

"How did your phone call go?"

Chris dropped his head and began shaking it.

"That bad?"

"It ended up being pretty good," Chris explained. "But I made a big goof up."

Cedric stared at him and waited for him to continue.

"We were talking and she asked me about Keats."

"Ah, yes," Cedric said. "She loves the romantics. Did you remember what we discussed about him?"

"Of course not," Chris answered.

"Oh no."

Chris laughed. "It gets worse. I thought she said

'cleats'."

That cracked Cedric up.

"I thought she was taking an interest in football, so I spent twenty minutes explaining all the equipment."

Cedric began laughing harder.

"She waited until I finished to correct me," Chris said. "Then she laughed about as hard as you are right now. By then it was time for us to get off the phone and get ready for bed. She ended by saying it was the best conversation she had ever had."

"Only you, my friend," Cedric said. "Only you can mess up so badly and come out smelling like a rose."

Chris puffed his chest out looking cocky.

"Tomorrow night is the play," Cedric said. "Have you thought about what you might say if you see her? She will certainly be there."

"Oh, that's what I came in to tell you. I can't make it. My dad's uncle died and we're leaving this morning to drive to Raleigh."

"I'm sorry to hear that," Cedric said.

"Thanks. So I wanted to ask if you could keep an eye on Roxy. You know, sit with her maybe and make sure no one else tries to move in on me."

Cedric looked at Chris with earnest eyes. "Oh that's asking an awful lot, but for you I will do it."

***

"Oh my goodness. I think the entire town is out there."

Roxy walked over beside Roger and peeked through the narrow divide in the stage curtains. "Looks like it. You're a star, Roger. Everyone has been dying to see your play. It's the talk of the town."

"Really?" Roger finally turned from the curtains. "I hope everyone likes it."

"I'm sure they will."

Roger continued to pace in a circle with his hands stuck deep in the pockets of his jeans. He was nervous to the point of being nauseated. He had written a few short plays that were performed in class, but never something that had drawn such an audience. Then he saw a familiar face approaching that put him more at ease. "Cedric. You made it."

Cedric walked up with a smile and a nod. "I wouldn't miss it for the world, my friend. It's an absolute masterpiece."

"You've read it?" Roger asked.

"Of course I have. It's your best work. You are truly a genius. But I am a little surprised you didn't get the fair maiden Roxy here to play the leading female role."

Roger nodded. "I wrote that part with her in mind. I mean, no one else could play Henrietta. But I couldn't persuade her."

Roxy smiled and shrugged her shoulders. "Now how could I ever watch and enjoy the play if I'm in it?"

"A very good point, my lady," Cedric said. "It's too bad Chris couldn't be here."

Roxy nodded in agreement. "Yes, but I will tell him all about it when he calls tonight."

"Of course," Cedric said.

Enter Madison stage left wearing a beautiful flowing gown. "Hey guys. How do I look?"

"Wonderful," Roxy said.

"Wonderful," Roger echoed.

"You are a true vision, dear," Cedric added.

"I'm so excited and a little scared. I just wanted to thank you again, Roger, for choosing me to play Henrietta. I was pleasantly surprised."

Roger looked briefly at Roxy and Cedric before commenting. "Well I wrote that part with you in mind, Madison. I mean, no one else could play that part. Come; let's see if everyone else is ready."

Roger and Madison walked away as Roxy and Cedric snickered.

Yet another familiar face made an appearance. It was Mannie Flarity, the male cheerleader. He wore his dress costume for the play.

"Hey, Roxy." Then he saw Cedric and his smile disappeared. "Oh no. Cedric. I didn't see you there."

"Yes, I get that a lot," Cedric said.

"Is it okay that I'm in the play?" Mannie asked.

Cedric laughed. "Of course, my friend." He walked over and put his arm around Mannie's shoulder, causing the poor boy to cower. "I know for a fact that Roger created that part just for you. Seriously, who else could play that part?"

"Really?"

"Absolutely, my dear friend. Now go break a leg."

Mannie breathed a sigh of relief, which reflected in a huge grin, and walked away.

Cedric looked at Roxy. "What part is he playing?"

Roxy laughed and punched Cedric in the chest.

"You're horrible. So, are you going to sit with me or not?"

"I don't wish to make all the other females in town jealous, but I hate to see you sit alone. Not to mention Chris ordered me to keep the guys away from you while he's away."

Roxy giggled. She walked down the steps on the side of the stage and Cedric followed. She walked only a short distance to the third row and saw two empty seats in the middle. "What about there?" she asked.

Cedric scanned the situation. The rows of seats were very close together. He would have to squeeze between at least a dozen people, and even if they stood to let him pass, he was sure to belly-bump everyone on that row and the row in front of them. He simply stared with a pitiful expression.

Roxy picked up on his anxiety. "You know what? This is way too close. There's a lot more space near the back."

Cedric smiled and followed her to the back where only a few people occupied seats. They sat in the middle of the next to last row with empty seats behind, beside, and in front of them. The metal folding chair squeaked in protest as Cedric eased his enormous frame into it. This was more like it. Plenty of room and no one around to complain.

It didn't last. Two middle school boys, about thirteen years old, came in and sat right behind them.

"Oh great," one of them said. "We can't see around the Great Wall of China."

The other boy laughed.

Cedric's jaw muscles tightened.

The two boys got up, walked around, and sat in the two seats right in front of Cedric and Roxy.

The same boy who made the comment puffed his chest out and pushed both arms out on each side of him. It was clearly an attempt to appear as a heavy person.

Roxy reached over and patted Cedric on the thigh as if to say she was proud of him for restraining.

Cedric simply smiled and looked straight ahead. Then he raised his right hand and thumped the boy on the back of the head. It landed so hard that it rang out like a watermelon.

"Ow!" the boy yelled and turned around. "What do you think —" Perhaps it was only then did he realize who it was that was sitting behind him. He faked a laugh. "Uh, we're going to sit somewhere else." He pushed his friend and they got up and walked closer to the front.

"You're incorrigible," Roxy said.

Cedric shrugged. "That's what everyone says about the Great Wall."

Roxy smiled and shook her head.

The lights dimmed and the curtain on the stage slid open. The first act of Roger's play began.

Cedric had read the play and knew what to expect, but still greatly enjoyed the performance as it played out. About halfway through the first act, he glanced over and noticed Roxy was reading the program. He thought that odd but focused again on the play.

When the second act began, he really paid attention because he had a feeling that Roger had used him for inspiration. It was a loose interpretation of *The Hunchback of Notre-Dame*. The hero, Bartholomew, who could have just as easily been named Quasimodo, is deformed from a farming accident, but falls for the beautiful princess Henrietta, played of course by Madison. The plot pivots around Bartholomew trying desperately to get the princess to see beyond his physical deformities and love him for who he is.

In fact, it hit so close to home that Cedric became uncomfortable watching it with Roxy. He looked over to see her reaction, but found her still reading the program. He knew something wasn't right.

He reached over and pulled the hidden sheet of paper out of Roxy's program.

"Hey," she said a little too loudly as several people in front of them turned back to look.

Cedric looked at the paper and found it to be a letter from Chris, a letter he himself had written. He shook his head and handed it back to her. "Now who's incorrigible?"

Roxy put the letter in her purse and watched the rest of the play.

Afterward, the two of them walked over to the Frosty Freeze and sat at a table. Roger's mom was behind the register instead of in the kitchen like she normally was. One of Roger's sisters came to take their order.

Roxy ordered a piece of pie and milk.

"What for you?" the waitress asked.

Cedric looked up. "Oh, I'm not hungry. Thanks."

Of course that wasn't true. He was always hungry.

Roger rushed in on Cloud Nine. "What did y'all

think?" he yelled before he even got to their table.

"Bravo," Cedric said.

"Great," Roxy added. "I was in tears. But why aren't you still with the cast for the curtain call?"

"Are you kidding?" he asked. "Do you know how busy we're about to be?" He walked over and took his mother's place and she went back to the kitchen.

He was right. Within ten minutes dozens of theater patrons filled the place.

Madison came in and sat with Cedric and Roxy. Her face was red from where they scrubbed off her makeup. "Well, how was I?"

They gave her the same responses they had offered to Roger.

"Wasn't it a great story?" she asked while she waved at Roger.

"It was," Roxy agreed.

"Roger did a fantastic job," Madison continued. "His writing is so good. That's what made it so believable."

"Believable?" Cedric blurted out before thinking. Roxy and Madison stared.

"You didn't find the story believable?" Roxy asked.

Cedric considered whether he should go on, but he had started it, so on he went. "I'm sorry, but that's not how it works in real life. A woman never sees the inner person if the outer person looks so horrible. The same would go for a man."

"But," Madison protested, "his looks were not his fault."

"Oh, so that is the standard?" Cedric asked. "If a person's deformity was caused by an accident, it makes it invisible to others? That would mean that if a person's horrible physical appearance were caused by their own hand, that person would not deserve the same consideration? Have I gotten it right?"

Madison sat with her mouth open. It was very probable that she finally understood that Cedric was referring to himself. "Uh… I need a drink." She got up and went to the counter and asked Roger for a Coke.

"You're in a mood tonight," Roxy said. "Are you still upset about me reading Chris's letter during the play?"

"No, of course not. It just gets to me how people love to claim that they see only the inner person. It is a distortion of reality."

"Really?" Roxy said. "I'd like to think I see only the inner person in people."

Cedric smiled a fake smile. "I guess it was lucky that you could see Chris's inner person past his ugliness."

Roxy smiled and shook her head. "Granted, Chris is very handsome. To say I don't see that would be a lie. But as I told you, I saw his true self in his eyes. Don't you believe you can find the truth if you look deep into someone's eyes?"

"Yes, Roxy, I do." Cedric stared longingly into the eyes of the girl he loved for so long.

Roxy stared back into his, first as a jest, and then she quickly looked down.

Cedric continued looking at her.

After a few seconds Roxy looked back up. "Cedric, I—"

"Help! Someone help!"

Cedric and Roxy both jumped. They searched to find the source of the piercing plea. A woman was standing and waving her hands frantically.

"He's choking," she continued.

Cedric saw a man, presumably her husband, slamming his fist into his own chest and trying hard to breathe.

"Somebody get a doctor," someone yelled.

Two men were slapping the guy on the back in an attempt to dislodge whatever was stuck in the guy's throat. That's all they could do because the man was very heavy.

Cedric sprang out of his chair, rushed over, and pushed the other men out of the way. He grabbed the guy under the armpits, locked his hands in front of him, and hoisted him completely out of the chair and off the floor. He maneuvered his fists down to the area below the ribs and pumped with all his might.

Please don't let me break his ribs, Cedric thought to himself.

The people who were gathered around could only watch in horror.

Cedric pumped again and a chunk of a chicken finger flew all the way across to the adjoining table. He sat the guy back in the chair.

"Are you okay?" the wife asked as she knelt beside him.

He nodded as his face slowly returned to the normal color. He looked back at Cedric. "Thank you, young man. You saved my life."

"You're welcome." Cedric patted him on the shoulder and turned to walk away.

"Hey," the guy said.

Cedric stopped and looked back.

The guy took a deep breath. "You think we're going to go all the way this year?"

Cedric laughed. "I should have left the chicken in you." He turned to look for Roxy but she was gone. He walked to the door, looked outside, but all he could see was darkness. He stared at his shoes and wondered what he had done. He pulled open the door and left.

CHAPTER TEN

———◆◆◆———

Cedric lay in bed that night as his thoughts betrayed him. He felt his life was so much better than it had ever been. He loved being a senior and playing football. He enjoyed working with Chris. And most importantly, he loved how much time he and Roxy shared. But he kept reliving that moment from last night when Roxy looked into his eyes and he forgot to hide the truth. Had he blown it? Was it all over? Would she ignore him now? Would she be too embarrassed to be around him?

He couldn't bear the possibility. That was all he had in life. His home life was basically nonexistent. Neither he nor his mom ever invited people over. He didn't want them to know where and how he lived. Well, everyone but Chris who often gave him a ride, but he never let him come inside.

He stared at the cracks in the ceiling, the old plaster deteriorating over the years to resemble a giant spider web, complete with images of hideous monsters scattered throughout. These images had so traumatized him as a child. Many nights he crawled out of bed and tiptoed down the hall to the door of his parents' bedroom. There he would fall asleep on the floor, which oftentimes drove his father into a rage if he was discovered.

One night Cedric finally made friends with the monsters, named them even. It was the night that it dawned on him that he was one of them, at least judging by his classmates in elementary school. The only thing worse than them calling him names was when they finally realized the dangers involved and shunned him altogether.

Roxy had always been the one bright spot through it all. But even Roxy, after Cedric rescued her in third grade, still gravitated to her own group of friends. She always acknowledged Cedric, and even smiled, but he was clearly not part of her circle.

When he started playing football in junior high school, that filled a huge void. Finally he had an outlet for his pent-up hostility. After all, not only was he applauded for his aggression, he was rewarded for it.

He reached down beside him and felt with his hand until he heard the container rattle in the darkness and brought up an Oreo-like cookie, only a cheaper version, and slid it between his lips.

After another thirty minutes he knew it was no use. He got up and walked into the kitchen and sat at the table in the dark. But still the anticipation persisted, the not knowing what would transpire between Roxy and him tomorrow at school. He knew now he would not sleep the entire night and decided if he must be awake, why not be productive?

He walked into his bedroom and fumbled through the stacks of books on the floor. At least 200 books adorned each wall of his bedroom, and more were stuffed under his bed. He searched until he found one of his favorites: *Fahrenheit 451* by Ray Bradbury. Most of his favorites were either set in the future or stories about people traveling to the future. Perhaps it was his bitter past or unsatisfying present that made futuristic books appeal to him. He opened and started to speedread.

He was halfway through the book in one hour's time. He worried not about missing any details since he knew the story by heart. He knew almost every book in his room by heart.

Placing a napkin between the pages to mark his spot, he decided to make this sleepless night even more productive. He walked to the fridge, opened it, and pulled out the bologna and cheese.

Cedric never tried to sleep again; he just sat there all night alone with his thoughts staring at the wall and the clock until time to get ready for school. Finally the time came and he showered and got dressed.

It was a chilly morning and drizzling rain as Chris came by to get him.

"How'd you sleep?" Chris asked as Cedric got into the car.

"Like a baby."

"That's good."

Cedric nodded. "Yes, I was up crying every fifteen minutes."

"Where do you get these things?" Chris asked with a chuckle.

"It's a side effect from reading."

Chris nodded. "I've got to try it sometime."

"Yes, you do, my friend. In fact, how far along are you on that list of books I provided to you?"

"I pinned it to my corkboard."

Cedric mumbled under his breath.

"You don't really expect me to read all those, do you?" Chris asked.

"I do, indeed. And then I expect you to ask me for another list. Have you ever thought about what will happen after you win Roxy's heart?"

Chris looked confused. "What do you mean?"

Cedric looked straight ahead as he answered. "Being an intellectual is not a goal or a destination; it's a journey. You cannot approach this thinking you only have to learn enough to impress the fair maiden. Once you have her, you might want to keep her. If and when you guys become a couple, you will be spending a lot of time together. What are your plans for that contingency?"

"I never thought about it like that," Chris admitted. "I just figured we would be kissing all the time."

Cedric shot a glance at Chris.

"I see your point," Chris said.

"What amazes me," Cedric said, "is how anyone could not have read these books, or many others like them. I mean, what were you doing with all your time as a teenager?"

Chris shrugged. "I don't know. Going to parties, going to dances, going to proms, going to movies, going to concerts, dating a lot, making out in the back seat, skinny-dipping a couple of times, boring stuff like that."

Cedric nodded and looked out the side window. "Well, when you put it that way, I guess if I had the chance to do those things, I never would have cracked open the first book either."

When they got to school they both went their separate ways.

Cedric sat through homeroom dreading the bell to ring to signify the start of his first class: English Lit. He shared that class with Roxy. He couldn't wish away the inevitable, however, and first period was announced with the screaming alarm.

He walked in and sat behind Roger, where he always sat. He glanced two rows over and noticed Roxy was not yet there.

"You look like death," Roger said after turning to look at Cedric.

"That's good because that's how I feel."

Roger looked up behind Cedric and smiled.

Cedric felt a hand slide across his back and shoulders. He flinched and then followed with his eyes as Roxy took her seat. She didn't seem upset.

After she positioned herself in her desk, she turned her head and smiled at Cedric. But it was a strange smile, devious and sneaky in appearance.

Cedric started to say something, but the school speakers came to life.

"Good morning, everyone. This is Principal Wilson with a special announcement. We have a hero in our ranks: our very own Cedric Deburr."

Cedric shot a stone-cold glance at Roxy, who shrugged and gave him a guilty look that said, "Who could have done such a thing?"

The principal continued. "Last night Cedric apparently remembered what he learned in Health class and used the Heimlich Maneuver and saved a man choking on a piece of food. Well done, Cedric."

The speaker went silent but the room erupted in applause.

"Did you really do that?" a female student asked.

"He did," Roger answered. "I saw it."

Cedric looked around at all the eyes on him. "Well, someone had to stop him from eating that food at the Frosty Freeze."

Everyone laughed.

***

Chris sat on his bed with the phone to his ear. Sheets of paper were scattered out all over his covers. He picked up one and read. "No, I don't think Shakespeare is overrated. I love his work. I actually think Macbeth is better than Hamlet. I know most people think Hamlet is his best work. I love a lot of his poetry too. Have you read *My Mistress' Eyes are Nothing Like the Sun*?"

Cedric looked on from the wooden chair.

Chris laughed. "No, I'm not going to recite it to you."

Cedric nodded in approval.

"Okay," Chris said. "I'm not sure I remember it all, but I'll try." He held up the sheet of paper and read.

```
    "My mistress' eyes are nothing
like the sun;
    Coral is far more red than her
lips' red;
```

If snow be white, why then her
breasts are dun;

If hairs be wires, black wires
grow on her head.

I have seen roses damasked, red
and white,

But no such roses see I in her
cheeks;

And in some perfumes is there
more delight

Than in the breath that from my
mistress reeks.

I love to hear her speak, yet
well I know

That music hath a far more pleas-
ing sound;

I grant I never saw a goddess go;

My mistress when she walks treads
on the ground.

And yet, by heaven, I think my
love as rare

As any she belied with false compare."

Cedric smiled. It was his favorite Shakespearean
poem.

"Which words?" Chris asked. "Oh, 'dun' means
off white and 'belied' means to compare." He was reading right from Cedric's notes.

Cedric was happy that Roxy was enjoying Chris's
intellect and creativity. After all, it was actually his own.

He continued to listen.

"Okay, I'll recite you one more poem today," Chris said. "But that's all. Do you know why rose bushes have thorns?"

Cedric smiled.

"I'm going to," Chris said as he picked up another sheet and read. "It's called Barbara Allen.

```
    It was in the fall of the year
    When  the  green  leaves  were  a
falling
    That Sir John Graeme in the west
country
    Fell in love with Barbara Allen

    He sent his men down to the town
    To the place where she was dwell-
ing
    Oh haste and come to our master
dear
    Gin you be Barbara Allen

    O Hooly, hooly rose she up
    To the place where he was lying
    And when she drew the curtain by
    'Young man, I think you're dy-
ing.'

    'O it's I'm sick, and very, very
sick
    And 'tis all for Barbara Allan
```

     O the better for me she'll never
be
     Tho my own heart's blood be
spilling'

     'O dinna ye mind, young man,'
said she
     'When the red wine you were fill-
ing
     And made the hearts gae round
and round
     But slighted Barbara Allan?'

     He turned his face unto the wall
     And death was with him dealing
     'Adieu, adieu, my dear friends
all
     And be kind to Barbara Allan.'

     And slowly, slowly rose she up
     And slowly, slowly left him
     Sighing said she could not stay
     Since death of life had reft him.

     She had not gane a mile but twa
     She heard the death-bell towing
     And every jow that the death-
bell geid
     It cried woe to Barbara Allan

     'O mother, mother make my bed

Make it saft and narrow
Since my love died for me today
I'll die for him tomorrow'

They buried her by the old church wall
And Sir Graeme was nigh her
From his grave grew a red, red rose
From her grave grew a brier

They grew to the top of the old church wall
Til they could grow no higher
There they tied a true love's knot
The red rose and the brier."

"What do you mean?" Chris asked then laughed. "Of course the brier would grow from *her* grave." He laughed again. "Okay, I'll talk with you tomorrow." He hung up the phone and lay back on the bed.

"Way to go, Romeo," Cedric said.

Chris sat back up. "But all we do is talk."

"You have to be patient. I don't think you're ready for a real date."

"But when?" Chris asked. "You know who's been asking her out lately and even showing up at her house?"

Cedric did indeed know: Anthony Royal, the mayor's son.

Chris continued. "How do I know she even likes

me? Maybe she likes him. She could just be messing with me. You're her friend, Cedric; you could find out. You can take my car."

He knew Cedric didn't have a car. In fact, neither did Cedric's mother.

"It's crazy," Cedric said. As he sat there, however, he began to have doubts himself. "Okay, I'll see if I can find out anything."

Chris handed his car keys toward Cedric. "Now be subtle about it."

Cedric stood up and reached for the keys.

"Be smart about it," Chris added.

Cedric grunted and snatched the keys from Chris's hand. He went out to the car and drove to Roxy's neighborhood but parked a block away so she wouldn't see the car. He walked to the house and knocked on the door.

Roxy answered. "Hey. What are you doing here?" She hugged her friend.

"In the neighborhood. Thought I would say hello."

"Why don't we sit out here? My mom and dad are playing cards with the neighbors."

There were several concrete garden statues along with the benches in front of the house, so they sat on one of the benches.

"What a nice surprise," Roxy said. "And what a beautiful fall day."

Cedric looked at the blue sky. "It is indeed."

"What a wonderful senior year this has turned out to be," Roxy said. "The football season is shaping up like everyone hoped, you are making the school proud with your math accomplishments, and I have never been happier."

"Ah yes," Cedric said. "Speaking of that, how are things going with Chris?"

Roxy looked surprised that Cedric knew what she was referring to. "Great. Why do you ask?"

"Oh, you know," Cedric said, "he told me you have been talking on the phone."

"Well," Roxy said, "if you must know, he's incredible. We talk for hours. He takes my breath away."

"So, he *is* this deep intellectual you thought he was?

Roxy blushed. "He's more than I ever dreamed. He has read so much and can converse on a multitude of subjects. But sometimes..."

"What?"

Roxy shrugged. "I wonder sometimes if he's talking to another girl."

"Why?"

"It's just that sometimes when we're talking, he gets quiet. He doesn't say anything for several seconds. It's almost as if he suddenly didn't understand what we were talking about. I think he's just distracted by something else, or someone else."

Cedric shook his head. "I don't think that's it."

"You're probably right," Roxy said. "He always snaps out of it and says something absolutely brilliant."

"Brilliant, huh?"

Roxy nodded.

"I understand you guys write letters, too. How is

his writing?"

"Better than yours," Roxy said.

Cedric smiled.

"Don't be jealous. His writing is better than anyone's I've ever read: Shakespeare, Keats, Hemmingway, Twain, or anyone."

"Wow," Cedric said. "That's impressive."

"He's a genius," Roxy added.

Cedric chuckled. "Oh come on. A genius?"

"I'm serious," Roxy said. "He might be the best writer in the world."

"Okay, if you insist."

"Okay, wise guy, listen to this. 'It is not truth I seek, nor faith, nor even God. It is the feeling in my heart when I think of you, a life-saving food source I never knew I needed, and like a slow moving river of hot lava, it cools my soul.'"

"It's kind of cute, I guess," Cedric said. "A little over the top, though, wouldn't you say?"

Roxy shook her head. "How about this one? 'I watched the bird scratching on the ground. And that was me looking for you. I watched the bird jump around. And that was me when I found you. I watched the bird stretch out its wings. And that was how large my world had become. I watched the bird soar into Heaven like a silver dart. And that... oh that was my heart.'"

"Kind of corny, don't you think?" Cedric asked.

"You're horrible," Roxy said. "You think just because a guy is physically attractive, he has to be a moron."

"That's not true. Well, mostly not true."

Roxy scoffed. "Just like every blond is an airhead,

right?"

"I have never thought that at all," Cedric answered.

"Good," Roxy said, "Want to hear more?"

"You have them all memorized?"

"Every one."

"Wow," Cedric said. "That's kind of flattering."

Roxy smiled. "I told you he's a genius."

"Well, how many feats of literary genius must this Roman god of poetry write before you actually go out with him?"

"I'm not sure," Roxy said. "I'm actually kind of nervous about that."

"Why?"

"I don't know how to explain it," she said. "You know how you read a great book that moves you very much?"

Cedric nodded.

"And then you see the movie and it's horrible?"

Cedric smiled. He knew that feeling very well. "So you're afraid reality might not compare to your fantasy?"

"Yeah, I guess so," Roxy answered. "But there's no hurry. We have the rest of our lives to figure it out."

"I suppose so," Cedric said. "So the next time you guys speak on the phone, what would you like to talk about?"

"Anything. And everything. I love when Chris describes his feelings for me using beautiful metaphors. They're just plain simple words that in reality mean nothing, but in my heart mean everything. I'll ask him why he loves me, how he loves me, and for how long will he love me." She crossed her arms across her belly and took a deep breath. She smiled at Cedric then looked serious. "But you won't tell him, will you?"

"I'm insulted."

Roxy giggled.

"Well, I better be going." As Cedric got up to leave, a red Ferrari pulled up in front of Roxy's house and Anthony Royal got out.

He seemed very surprised to see Cedric. "Hey, Roxy. You look great today." Then, almost as an after-thought and in a very flat tone: "Uh, Cedric."

Cedric walked quickly over to Anthony so fast it made Anthony take a step back. "It's good to see you, Anthony. You look great today." Then he turned toward Roxy and in a flat tone said, "Uh, Roxy."

Roxy laughed out loud.

Anthony stood there befuddled as Cedric walked away.

CHAPTER ELEVEN

Cedric stood on the sidelines and looked at the play clock on the scoreboard. There were only a few minutes left to go. Most games were on Friday night, but this one was a rare Saturday afternoon game. His hair was soaked with sweat. Unlike other players who seemed comfortable to keep their helmets on, Cedric took his off every chance he got. He sweated so much it was hard to see at times. The score stood 28 – 0. His night was finished as the coach decided to let his second string get some experience with the outcome certainly decided. It was the last game of the season and the eleventh win in a row for the Cavaliers. The season was indeed shaping up like the town had hoped it would with a perfect season. Next would be the state playoffs. It was also the last game before Christmas break. Cedric stole a glance at the cheerleaders, his focus zeroing in on Roxy of course.

Roxy's golden curls danced and seemed to give off their own light as she bounced up and down in the sunshine. She was truly a vision.

Cedric walked back to the bench, grabbed a cup of Gatorade, and walked to the end closest to the cheerleaders and sat. All seemed right with the world. He was doing well in school, in football, and spending more time with Roxy than he ever thought possible. No one from school ever made fun of him anymore, at least not to his face. It was a feeling he had never experienced, a feeling of acceptance.

"Hey 69."

Cedric looked around to find Chris. It was common for players to call each other by their number instead of their name. Cedric often joked that he picked 69 in case he was ever knocked upside down it wouldn't matter since the number would remain the same. The joke was really that Cedric had never been knocked down before, not in football or in a fight.

"Hey, Chris. You did well tonight."

Chris took a seat beside Cedric. He had proven a valuable addition to the team. Many games he started either as a receiver or in the backfield of the defense. The coach had learned that he could use Chris in a multitude of positions. Chris had good hands and had already caught several touchdown passes in the new season, knocked down several passes while playing cornerback, and had one interception.

"We still on for tonight?" Chris asked.

"You bet."

Cedric had been coaching Chris at a totally different game: trying to win Roxy's heart. And it appeared to be working. He would write beautiful love letters and Chris would sign them and mail them to Roxy or have someone pass them to her in school. The nights Chris called Roxy, Cedric would write down things for Chris to say as they spoke on the phone, like little poems and information about books and other things he knew would impress Roxy.

Sometimes on the phone Roxy would ask questions that caught Chris off guard and he would panic and freeze or tell her his mom was calling and he had to go. But he was getting so much better with conversation.

"Guess what I did?" Chris asked.

"Went to the bathroom by yourself?"

Chris laughed. "No. I've been doing that since I was 15."

Cedric's eyes got wide. "Am I losing my mind or are you developing a sense of humor?"

"You're rubbing off on me I guess," Chris said. "I've cleared off a spot on my shelves for a math trophy."

Cedric took his jersey to wipe away the sweat, and to hide his smile.

"No," Chris said, "I read one of your books on the list: *The Time Machine*."

"Very good. How did you like it?"

"I loved it, except for the ending. Do you think he went back and spent the rest of his life with Edwina?"

"Maybe," Cedric answered. "But that's the genius of great writers. They use the most powerful tool in literature: the reader's imagination. So the question is: Is that what you think the time traveler did?"

Chris nodded. "Yep. I think he went back to Edwina, got married, had kids, and built a 7-Eleven and lived happily ever after."

Cedric chuckled. "Could be. Personally I think he accidentally went back in time and was eaten by a T-Rex."

"Yes, that sounds like you, always the eternal optimist."

Cedric looked at Chris with surprise. "Those are some mighty big words you're using these days."

"Well, a sophisticated mind of logic espires... aspires..."

Cedric doubled over with laughter. "A man has got to know his limitations."

"Wait," Chris said. "That's a Dirty Harry quote. You said you didn't watch movies."

"It was a novel series first, goofball."

"Oh, I knew that."

"So, are you ready for tonight?" Cedric asked.

Chris looked at Roxy cheering with the squad and shook his head. "Absolutely not at all. I'm going to fall flat on my face. I know it."

Cedric tried to provide encouragement. "Don't worry; you're ready."

The final whistle blew and the game was over. They shook hands with the opponents and headed to the dressing rooms to hear the coach give his standard congratulatory speech, with the added sentiments of finishing the season undefeated and headed to the playoffs.

Chris drove Cedric home after they showered and changed. They sat in the car for a while as Cedric gave him last-minute advice. Normally Chris would be calling Roxy but this night was special. Chris and Roxy would have their first ever real date at the Frosty Freeze. Chris was nervous to say the least.

"Aww, man," Chris said. "I'm so gonna blow it."

"You're not going to blow it," Cedric said. "Let's

go over the news and the books we've been studying."

Cedric pretended to be Roxy and asked Chris all sorts of questions. Chris knew this was important because in all the letters Roxy had written back to him, she must have asked a hundred questions about current events, literature, and a multitude of other subjects. Luckily it was easy to respond to those questions with Cedric in his corner, but this night he would be on his own.

Cedric asked several questions they had practiced, but decided to throw a curve ball. "Could you believe the stock market dropped over 22 percent in one day? What do you think caused it?"

Chris took on the look of a deer caught in the headlights. "Uh… Well. It uh… "

Cedric rolled his eyes. "Say something for Pete's sake."

Chris nodded. "I've been so busy with football that I haven't really followed the news lately. What do you think happened?"

"That's good," Cedric said. "That's very good. It's a viable excuse and you turned it around to put the question on her. Obviously she has an opinion on it or she wouldn't bring it up."

Chris looked confused. "So the stock market really dropped?"

Cedric dropped his head into his hands and looked back up. "Yes. You're killing me." Cedric asked Chris several more questions then threw another curveball, which once again stumped Chris.

Chris threw his hands in the air. "I give up."

"Dang it; remember your safe answers," Cedric demanded.

"Oh yeah. Uh… I really don't know. I'm afraid I don't have all the answers."

Cedric nodded. "Don't be afraid to use that. Roxy loves intelligence, but she also loves honesty. Now what's your other safe line in case the conversation gets too deep?"

"Oh," Chris said, "Uh… Can't I just enjoy sitting with you here for a moment?" He spoke in a monotone as he searched his memory for the words.

"Goodness gracious," Cedric barked. "Do you think you could possibly say that with any less emotion? Seriously, give it a little meaning, any meaning."

"Okay, okay. I'm sorry. Let me try it again."

"And remember the goal."

Chris nodded. "I know. Ask her to wear my class ring."

"Exactly," Cedric said. "Personally I think it's a foolish gesture, but that seems to carry some weight with the derelict masses of high school robots. And it will let you know right away where Roxy stands, and more importantly, let Anthony Royal know where Roxy stands."

Chris spun his ring around his finger. "That's an awful amount of weight to put on such a small… uh, device."

"Device?"

"Uh… contraption?"

Cedric shook his head.

"Thingie?" Chris asked.

"There you go."

They continued to practice up until 5:00. Chris drove home and got ready then came back to pick up Cedric. Cedric rode with Chris and had him drop him off around back.

"Remember," Cedric said, "only in an extreme situation can we do this, but I'll be back here the entire time. If you get stuck, excuse yourself to go to the bathroom and come back here. But you can only do this once. We don't want her thinking you have a medical disorder." Cedric laughed.

Chris gulped and drove around to the front. He went in and took a seat by the entrance and waited. Several times he dried his hands on his jeans. He felt a little uncomfortable in the button-collar shirt and button-up sweater, but Cedric had picked out the attire.

"Hey, Chris. Waiting on someone?"

Looking up to see Roger, Chris nodded.

"Great game today," Roger said. "I think this is our year."

"I hope so," Chris said and felt a little better to get his mind off Roxy.

Roger waved and went back to work.

"Hey."

Chris almost jumped out of the chair. Roxy had walked in without him noticing. She wore a dark sweater that made her hair stand out. Chris now realized Cedric knew what he was doing in the wardrobe department. "Shall we get a table?"

Roxy nodded and they walked to an empty table as Chris pulled the chair out for her then took the seat across from her.

"You look great today," Chris said.

Roxy smiled. "Thanks. Great game today. How many passes did you catch?"

Chris felt the excitement rise inside of him. He loved to talk about his achievements in sports and about sports in general. But he sensed something else, a presence on his shoulder like a little angel, or perhaps more like a little demon. It was the voice of Cedric saying, "Whatever you do, don't talk about playing football or anything related to sports."

"Well?" Roxy asked in his silence.

Chris shrugged. "I'm not sure. We all had a good day so I'm happy for the team and the town. I'd rather talk about you."

Roxy giggled.

The waitress, one of Roger's sisters, brought the menus so the first few minutes were easy as they simply looked to see what they wanted to eat and gave her the order.

After she left – silence.

"You look great," Chris said, suddenly remembering his opening line but not remembering he had already used it.

"Still?" Roxy asked and smiled.

"Steel?" Chris asked. He was confused.

Roxy shook her head. "You told me that just a few moments ago. I'm glad I haven't changed in that time."

Chris blushed. "Sorry. I'm just nervous. But there is something I wanted to say."

"What?"

"You look great today."

Roxy giggled again. "That's so original. Thank you. And you too."

Chris smiled and nodded.

"Which reminds me," Roxy said, "great game today?"

"Okay, you got me. And yes, it was a great game. Could be our year."

Roxy smiled. "You think so?"

Chris shrugged. "Well, I've heard other people say that."

"So our first official date," Roxy said. "Looks like you picked the right spot."

Chris was caught off guard. Was she serious? Was she joking? Was it sarcasm? "We can go somewhere else if you'd like."

"No. I was kidding. This is perfect. Where else would we go in Frenchtown?"

Chris thought hard but didn't know the answer. He had not been here long and this was the only place he had eaten outside the school and his home. "Uh—"

"It's a rhetorical question, Chris."

Rhetorical? Chris searched his memory. He knew he had heard Cedric use that word.

Roxy must have picked up on his confusion. "It's a question that doesn't require an answer."

"Oh yeah," Chris said. "Those are my favorites."

Roxy laughed.

Everything was going well, but then it got serious.

"I love your letters," Roxy said. "I love the way you write. You know so much about great literature. And your own writings, especially the poems, are wonderful. From where do you get your ideas?"

Chris's heart rate began to increase. "Uh... Well, I really don't know. I mean I don't have all the answers."

He couldn't believe he had to use one of his safe lines right off the bat, and, judging from the expression on Roxy's face, it wasn't the best time. He quickly fell back on what Cedric had taught him: to turn the table and ask her questions.

"So, have you lived here all your life?"

Roxy smiled and nodded.

"What are your plans after school?" he asked.

"College."

Several seconds of silence followed as Chris hoped the food would soon arrive.

Roxy broke the silence. "The springtime pedals poem you wrote about me, was it based on a famous novel?"

Chris tried to think of the poem Cedric had written. "A little, I guess."

Roxy looked perplexed again. "Does this question bother you?"

"No, not at all," Chris offered but not very convincingly. "Can I just enjoy being here with you?" There went the last safe line, and like the first, at the absolute wrong time.

"I'm sorry," Roxy said. "I didn't realize talking about your writing would not be enjoyable. I would have thought writers love to talk about their prose. It means a lot to me and I just wanted you to know that."

"Oh no... I mean... yeah, that's nice. Uh... I just

meant… uh… "

Roxy looked down as if she was embarrassed to look at him or perhaps felt guilty for offending him.

Chris was completely lost, so he did the only thing he could think to do. "Will you excuse me while I go to the restroom?"

"Of course," Roxy answered.

Cedric looked up from his bench in disbelief as Chris exited the back door then he looked down at his watch. "You have to be kidding me."

"It's horrible," Chris said as he sat beside Cedric. "I am so stupid. You have to get me out of this."

"How can I do that?"

"I don't know," Chris said, "but you have to think of something. I'm blowing it big time."

"Okay," Cedric said. "Get back in there and I'll come around front."

Chris walked back inside and back to the table. "Sorry," he said as he took his seat.

"Are you okay?" Roxy asked.

"Just been feeling a little bad today."

"I didn't know," Roxy said. "We could have done this another night."

Cedric came in the front entrance. "Oh, there you are." He walked up and sat at the table with Roxy and Chris.

"Hey, Cedric. What are you doing here?" Roxy asked.

"I came to find Chris. Chris, it's your dad. Your mom called me and asked me to find you."

"My dad?" Chris asked.

Cedric nodded. "Yeah, you better go check on him."

Chris looked at Roxy.

"Yes, of course," Roxy said. "Go. I'll be fine."

Chris nodded and started out the door. Then he went back and laid a twenty dollar bill on the table and left again.

"What's going on?" Roxy demanded.

Cedric lied some more. "His father has been sick all day but it suddenly took a turn for the worse. They might have to take him to the hospital. Poor Chris has been worried all day. He can't even think straight."

"Oh my goodness," Roxy said. "I knew something was bothering him. I was so mean and I feel like a horrible person."

At that moment the waitress brought out the food, the order originally meant for Roxy and Chris.

Cedric picked up a fork. "Don't beat yourself up about it. Let's eat."

Roxy laughed and began to eat as well.

Cedric was really enjoying himself. They ate and talked about whatever subject Roxy wanted to talk about.

A few moments later, three of his football teammates came in. Seeing Cedric with Roxy, they decided to have some fun and sat at the table next to them.

"No wonder Cedric has no energy on the ballfield," one joked as he looked at the other two. "All his energy is going elsewhere."

The others laughed. One made kissing motions on his hand.

"So, Cedric," the third said, "after you tutor me in

math, can you tutor me in love?"

Roxy and Cedric were getting a kick out of the jokes.

"It's my favorite Disney movie," the first one added, "Beauty and Debeast."

Cedric stopped smiling and turned to stare at the guy.

"Oh shoot," the guy said. "I didn't mean… uh, I meant the very handsome, totally in-shape beast." He stood and pointed toward the back. "We're going to go sit back there."

The trio quickly walked away as the other two laughed heartily at the first one's near blunder.

Cedric looked back at Roxy, smiled, and shrugged.

"I guess they think we're a couple," Roxy said.

Cedric's cheeks turned red. "You want me to go straighten them out?"

Roxy laughed. "Oh yes. I mean, how horrible that would be."

"Not for you," Cedric said. "I was thinking of me. You know I have a reputation to think of here."

"I'll try not to embarrass you and hopefully there will be no more Disney jokes made at our expense."

"Well," Cedric said, "I just thought he was a tad disrespectful. He had no right to call you 'Debeast'."

Roxy laughed very hard and slapped Cedric on the arm. "You're terrible."

Suddenly Cedric was glad Chris had messed up so badly. How else could he have ended up on a Saturday-night date with the girl he loves?

CHAPTER TWELVE

"Thanks for the lift." Cedric got out of Roxy's car and waved goodbye.

Roxy rolled down her window and waved as she drove away.

It had been a fun evening. He and Roxy talked about many different things, none of them being Chris. With her he felt at ease, at peace, but it was only because he knew there was one topic he would never discuss with her — his heart. His true heart. His true feelings. As long as Roxy was ignorant to that, he was safe in her presence. He was protected behind a thin veil of friendship and he could dazzle her with his wit and knowledge. It almost felt like a date. Almost.

The sliver of a moon barely cast any light on the ground, and Cedric's mom was no doubt already asleep and had left no lights on in or outside the house. He was still on Cloud Nine from his evening. He had not hoped for Chris to blunder his opportunity so badly, but all's well that ends well. He inhaled the crisp air and smiled. As he made his way to the front door, a voice in the darkness made him jump.

"Hey."

"Dang it, Chris. You scared the crap out of me.

What are you doing here?"

"I need to know what happened. Did I blow it?"

"No," Cedric said shaking his head. "I think I saved it for you. And it's more than you deserve. What were you thinking? After all the work we've put into this. How could you fail so miserably?"

"I know." Chris agreed. "But we're so close. I know if I ask, she will be my girl and wear my ring. I know I have no right to ask you after my actions tonight, but I am going to ask. I have to. Please? You have to help me. You have to fix this… tonight."

"Tonight? Are you crazy?"

"We have to," Chris pleaded. "Anthony Royal asked her to the prom last week, and she just told him she'd have to think about it. She didn't even say no. I'm running out of time. You have guided me this far. Let us finish this together. You have to help me win her over tonight. Please. I'm begging you."

Cedric stood there in the darkness wondering what to do. Part of him simply wanted to go to bed and call it a night. Part of him knew Chris was right. And part of him wanted to punch Chris for ruining his perfect evening. He took a deep breath. "Okay, let's go over there."

They got in Chris's car and drove to Roxy's house. All the lights were on, including the one in Roxy's room. They walked around to the side of the house underneath Roxy's bedroom on the second floor. All the homes in the neighborhood sported large yards so no other house was nearby.

Cedric walked back to the driveway, bent over,

and picked up some small pieces of gravel. He walked back and handed them to Chris. "Get her attention."

Chris tossed the first pebble and it landed against the glass of Roxy's window.

Nothing.

He tossed another and another.

The curtain opened. Chris and Cedric took a step back into the shadows.

Roxy lifted her window and stuck her head out. She was wearing pajamas. Her beautiful hair flowed with the night breeze. She squinted and looked downward. "Is someone out here?"

"It's me, Chris," he said softly.

"Chris? What are you doing down there?"

"I had to see you. I felt bad about tonight."

"It's okay, Chris. Cedric explained everything."

Cedric whispered in Chris's ear.

"It's not okay," Chris said, "because that's not the real issue."

Cedric whispered.

Chris repeated. "I've come here to ask for forgiveness and not just for tonight."

"For what then?" Roxy asked.

Cedric whispered.

"For not being one hundred percent honest. I came to tell you the whole truth."

Roxy cocked her head sideways and tried to peer into the darkness below. "Really? Then tell me the whole truth."

Cedric whispered in his ear.

"The truth is I'm a fool."

"Why?"

Cedric whispered.

"Because when I'm in your presence, my mind becomes as tangled as my voice."

Cedric whispered.

"I am so smitten, so in awe of you."

Cedric whispered.

"You're like a dream and I'm afraid you'll disappear like a miss."

"A miss?" Roxy asked. "What does that mean?"

Cedric grabbed Chris by the shoulders and whispered louder.

"A mist, Roxy," Chris corrected. "A mist."

Cedric whispered again.

"It's as if our relationship is a tiny sapling in a forest of giant redwoods."

Whisper.

"It needs cultivating to survive at this crucial juncture."

Whisper.

"And I feel like an amateur gardener not knowing how best to help it grow."

Whisper.

"What if I give it too much water? What if it doesn't get enough sunshine?"

Whisper.

"All I know for sure is that this little sapling…"

Whisper.

"Has the potential to be the most beautiful tree in the forest."

Whisper.

"In any forest."

Whisper.

"So I will give it my all, my best."

Whisper.

"Because I know this one tree carries two hearts."

Whisper.

"It carries our hearts, Roxy. Our dreams. Our future."

Roxy put her hand to her chest. "Yes, Chris. It must be a wonderful little tree. Tell me more about this precious plant. Tell me more about the future."

Whisper.

"Nothing else matters to me at this moment…"

Whisper.

"Than to give this sapling a chance to reach its potential."

Whisper.

"So that every other tree in the forest…"

Whisper.

"Will one day marvel at its strength and beauty."

"That's beautiful, Chris, and very nice to hear," Roxy said. "But you sound odd. Why does it take you so long to think of what to say?"

"This is not working," Cedric whispered. Staring up at Roxy in the window, he spoke louder. "I have to choose my steps carefully, like a treasure hunter seeking a golden chalice in a cave fraught with booby traps."

"What are you doing?" Chris whispered. He quickly looked up to see if Roxy was on to them.

"Go on," Roxy said.

Chris motioned with his hands. "Go on," he

whispered.

"One wrong word," Cedric continued, "is like making one wrong step, and the cave collapses around me, the journey and the dream might end."

"I can barely hear you," Roxy said. "Why don't you come closer?"

"No."

"Then I'll come down."

"No!"

"That was a mighty 'No,'" Roxy said. "Why not?"

"Let me speak to you for a moment from the safety of the night," Cedric said. "You don't have to see me to know my words are true, to know my feelings are real. You don't need your eyesight or any senses you might use to discover material things. You need only your heart to understand, to believe. Oh let me have this one chance to speak to you as me, with my own words and voice, to say the things I've dreamed of saying to you for so long. Give me this chance to see the journey to the end, to find and claim the treasure and make it mine."

"And what is the treasure?" Roxy asked, her hand still at her heart.

"You, my love. You are the treasure. Do you even know how incredible you are? A soul so pure and untainted. A spirit touched by the ancient goddesses of Rome. A heart so divine it makes the angels weep. You are a woman beyond the years of a schoolgirl, an anomaly with a gift to change the world. And who am I? Who is any guy that should ask you to be his?"

Roxy's hand moved to her neck as she stared at

the stars.

"You have become my everything, my all," Cedric continued. "Everything I see reminds me of you. Everything I hear; everything I taste. The other day I thought I heard your name, but when I turned around there was only a squirrel there. It made a chirping noise, but the longer I listened, I could tell it was chirping your name. 'Roxy. Roxy.' And soon my heart was syncing and each beat proclaimed your name. 'Roxy. Roxy.' And each pulse that pumped the blood through my veins echoed that beautiful word. 'Roxy. Roxy.'"

Roxy sighed. "Beautiful words. But you seem different. Even your voice has changed."

"Yes, it has changed. It's my voice; my true voice. No more hiding. I offer every ounce of courage I can muster. I speak to you tonight as if I speak to you for the first time. I speak to you with my heart and with my soul, not just the sounds coming from my lips. And you hear them. And you feel them, don't you?"

"Yes," Roxy said.

"And they move you. This is the night I have dreamed of, the night I can tell you how I feel and you hear the words and believe them. No more fear. No more doubt. I give you everything that I am and everything I ever hope to be. I can feel your heart in the darkness reaching all the way down where I stand. I am submerged yet freer than I ever have been before. Can you feel it, Roxy?"

"Yes," Roxy whispered. "I feel your words and I feel your heart. You have swept me off my feet with your wonderful words, and I am yours. I am forever yours."

"I have done this," Cedric said, "I and I alone. It is I who have made you tremble in the darkness. And you do tremble, don't you? It is my heart you have connected with. Mine and mine alone."

"Yes, Chris," Roxy said. "I do tremble and I do love you, and you have done this to me. I am coming down, Chris. I can't wait anymore." Roxy turned and dashed from the window. A moment later she came out the front door wrapped in a blanket.

"Go to her," Cedric whispered.

Chris walked up on the porch and took Roxy in his arms. As she stared into his eyes, she tiptoed toward his lips, and they kissed for the first time. The blanket fell to the porch.

Cedric watched from the darkness. He felt a sense of accomplishment but it was shared with a sense of regret. It was his words that won her. It was his words that she now kissed, but it was not on his lips.

Chris and Roxy walked into the house and closed the door behind them.

Cedric walked up on the porch and picked up the blanket and put it to his face. He was tired emotionally, more drained than he had ever felt, even after a football game. "I did it," he whispered. "I did it. But what did I do? Did I win or did I lose? But at least I have something I did not own before this night and that is something I never thought I would ever have." He looked around the neighborhood. He peered into the darkness of the trees across the street. He stared up at the heavens. The moment seemed to him surreal and yet he had no one to share it with, no one to confide in. He slowly walked down the steps and sat on the concrete bench and simply stared at the ground. He didn't know what emotions he felt.

Suddenly the headlights of a car appeared down the block. As it passed under a streetlight, Cedric recognized the red Ferrari. He knew it was a crucial juncture of Chris's and Roxy's relationship, and they needed a little time to seal their bond. He quickly devised a plan of distraction. He threw the blanket over his head and shoulders and waited for the intruder to come to him.

Anthony Royal parked his car and got out, reached back in and pulled out a bouquet of roses. He strolled with the confidence of a man clear about his purpose, sure of his outcome. He held the roses in front of him close to his chest. As he neared the steps, Cedric spoke.

"Beware, Anthony."

Anthony almost jumped out of his shoes. "What? Who's there?" He peered into the darkness.

"It is I," Cedric said.

Anthony walked over to the bench. In the dim light he could barely make out the person sitting there. "Who are you? What are you doing out here?"

"You sent me," Cedric said in a low voice. "You sent me to warn you."

Anthony seemed intrigued. "What does that mean: 'I sent you'? I don't know what you're talking about. How could I do that? When did I do that?"

"Thirty years from now," Cedric answered. "You sent me from the year 2017 with an urgent message. I came to warn you about your future and the future of your loved ones."

"You're drunk," Anthony said and turned to walk away.

"In two days' time," Cedric said a little louder, "your father will decide to run a story in his paper. You cannot allow that to happen."

Anthony stopped and turned around.

Cedric continued. "It will set in motion a series of events that will inevitably lead to his fall."

Anthony walked back. "'Fall'? What does that mean? What do you know of my father or his business? Do you mean the fall of his business or does he die? Tell me."

"His business will fall first."

"'First'? Tell me more. What is the story about? How do I even know you're telling the truth? "

Cedric looked slowly to his left and then to his right. "You must trust me. It involves a government official, a high ranking state official. The story is true, but it ends the career of an important man. There will be anger, retribution... blood. It is imperative that this story does not see the light of day or all will be lost forever."

Anthony rubbed his chin as if he was beginning to wonder if this mysterious person really was from the future. "Is it the governor?"

"No."

"The lieutenant governor?"

"No."

"Come on, dude. Tell me who it is."

"Guess," Cedric said.

"This is crazy. Just tell me."

"Guess."

Anthony shook his head and let out a deep breath. "I have no idea. Is it the Attorney General? Tell me the truth. And tell me how to stop my father from running the story."

Cedric waved his hand slowly in a large arch. "You will have to convince your father to change his course of action."

"How do I do that?"

Cedric looked left and right again to buy more time. "There's only one way."

"How? What is the way?"

Cedric pulled the blanket tighter around his face and shook his head.

Anthony lost his patience and forgot he was whispering. "Tell me, you idiot," he yelled.

The porch light came on and Anthony looked toward the steps to the porch. He stepped away from the mysterious person and approached the front of the house, still clutching the flowers in front of him.

Roxy and Chris came out of the door with their arms around each other. She was wearing Chris's class ring.

"What's going on here?" Anthony asked. He looked at Chris. "What are you doing here?"

Roxy was confused as well, especially when she recognized the shape of the person under the blanket. "Cedric?"

Anthony was already noticeably upset but became even more so when he saw Cedric. He yanked off the blanket. "You."

"Me," Cedric replied and stood.

"I should have recognized that body," Anthony snapped.

"Indeed," Cedric said.

"Can someone tell me what's going on?" Roxy asked.

"I should ask you the same thing," Anthony said. Then he noticed the ring on Roxy's finger. "I came to ask you again about going to the prom with me, but I see now you have just been toying with me."

"It's not like that," Chris said. "This just sort of happened."

"Well, congratulations to you both." Anthony's words dripped with sarcasm. He turned to look at Cedric. "And to you also, my time-traveling friend." He poked Cedric in the chest. "This is not over." He turned to walk away but turned back and stuck the flowers in Cedric's chest.

Cedric grabbed the bouquet and smiled.

At that Anthony turned and walked to his car, got in, and drove away.

Roxy looked at Cedric. "What are you doing here?"

"Oh, I was looking for Chris when I saw Anthony pull up. I was just having a little fun with him." He walked up and presented the roses to her. "I guess these are for you."

Roxy reluctantly took the bouquet and shook her head as if that might help clarify events. "I have to get some sleep, guys." Then she kissed Chris again. "I'll miss you."

"I can't believe I won't see you for an entire

week," Chris said.

"What does that mean?" Cedric asked.

Roxy hugged Chris then looked at Cedric. "I go to my grandmother's tomorrow."

Cedric nodded. He knew Roxy always went to spend a week with her grandmother in Tampa the first week of Christmas vacation.

Chris kissed her one more time and walked off the porch. "Get some sleep and have a good trip tomorrow."

Cedric and Chris walked toward his car.

"Cedric, wait," Roxy said.

Cedric walked back. "What is it?"

"I'm worried. Anthony seems pretty upset. Don't let anything happen to Chris."

"I'll try," Cedric said. "That's all I can say." He turned to walk away.

"Keep an eye on him please," Roxy pleaded.

"I'll do my best."

"Make sure he calls me every day,"

"I'll remind him."

"And make sure he writes to me too," Roxy called out.

Cedric stopped and turned to face her. "That I promise you."

He and Chris got in the car and drove away.

CHAPTER THIRTEEN

"As you know, gentlemen, this school hasn't been to the playoffs in over a decade. We haven't won a championship in several decades." The football coach walked up and down looking each player in the eyes. "Heck, I was only five years old when this school won its only state championship. We've practiced and played hard all season. This is our time. You guys have earned this."

The players all stood along the sidelines in their practice uniforms in full pads and helmets. It was indeed a big thing for the school and for the town, and every player felt the pride, especially Cedric.

"Look," the coach continued, "I don't want this for me. Well, that's not entirely true. I mean, if we win it all, maybe I'll get a real offer to coach a real team at a real school."

Everyone laughed.

"I want it for you guys. I want it for the town. I want it for every player who ever played for a small school that never got this chance. What do you say, guys? Do you want it?"

The team erupted in cheers.

For the next hour they practiced harder than ever. Cedric tried hard to shake the thoughts of Roxy, but to little avail.

Finally the coach called them all in. "Let's win this for Frenchtown."

The players all cheered again.

"Cap," the coach called out after the jubilation died down. "Take them for two laps around the field."

"Yes, sir," Cap said. "Let's go, boys."

Everyone fell in line behind Cap as he began to jog around the football field. Cedric and Chris brought up the rear.

"What a season, huh?" Chris said.

Cedric nodded.

"And that's not even the coolest thing that has happened," Chris added and looked over at Cedric as they ran.

Cedric simply nodded again. He knew to what Chris referred. As they made the circle on the end of the field near the parking lot, Cedric gasped.

"What's wrong?" Chris asked.

Cedric nodded toward the end zone at a person waving at them. "Chris, look."

Chris looked and saw what Cedric saw. It was Roxy waving in their direction. Chris was happy. "Hey, she came home a couple days early."

"This is bad," Cedric said.

"Why?"

"Uh, I meant to tell you something," Cedric said. "You wrote her a letter a few days ago."

"Okay," Chris said as they jogged. He didn't understand why that should be the cause of anxiety. He knew that Cedric usually let him read all the letters before he sent them to Roxy, but with her being out of town, time was of the essence. He trusted Cedric. "That's a good thing, right? I'm sure it was a great letter. That might be why she came home early."

Cedric nodded. He knew that's exactly why she had come home early and was suddenly worried sick. "Probably. I was just going to prep you for some of the things in the letter."

"Like what?" Chris asked. "Is there something different about this letter?"

"Not really," Cedric answered. "Well, it's kind of more of the same."

"Okay." Chris still couldn't understand.

"Well," Cedric said, "perhaps this one is a little more—"

"Stop the chatter," the coach yelled.

Cedric could say no more. They finished the two laps and the coach called them in for one last pep talk before releasing them. Practice ended and the players went to the dressing rooms to shower. Afterward Cedric and Chris walked to the parking lot.

Roxy was still there. She ran to Chris, threw her arms around him, and they kissed.

"Why are you home early?" Chris asked.

"It's your fault," Roxy said.

Chris forced a laugh. "My fault? I'm sure I'm innocent."

"Hey Cedric," Roxy said.

Cedric smiled and nodded.

She kissed Chris again. "Will you go somewhere with me?"

Chris nodded and turned and tossed Cedric his keys. "Take my car and I will pick it up later."

Cedric agreed, but was still very nervous.

Chris got into Roxy's car and she drove away.

"Where are we going?" Chris asked.

"You'll see."

Roxy drove to the rock quarry and parked. There were no other cars around. All the kids in town knew of this place, or at least of its reputation, even Chris. It was rumored to be the favorite place for the local teens to go parking.

Roxy leaned over and kissed Chris again.

"Are you going to tell me what's going on?" Chris asked. "Why did you come back so soon? Is your grandmother okay?"

"Yes, she's fine," Roxy said, "but I'm not."

"What?" Chris became concerned. "What happened?"

"Aren't you glad to see me?"

Chris smiled. "Of course I am."

"Like I said; it's your fault," Roxy said.

"I don't understand."

Roxy giggled. "Don't play coy. You know what you did and it was the most wonderful thing anyone has ever done for me."

Chris smiled but had no idea what she was talking about.

Roxy grabbed her purse from the back seat, pulled out an envelope, and handed it to Chris. "Your letter, silly."

Chris looked at the envelope and couldn't believe

it. It was a half inch thick. Cedric said he had written her a letter, not a book. He pulled out the letter and fumbled through it. It was fifteen pages long. "But I've written you love letters before."

"Not like this one," Roxy said.

Chris slowly read over the first page and was truly amazed. It was incredible. He had never read or heard anything like it. Cedric had impressed him many times in the last few months, but nothing had prepared Chris for this. He read the next page and started reading the third. Then he noticed little round stains on each page. Teardrops.

"What are you doing?" Roxy asked. "Have you already forgotten what you wrote?"

"It just reads so well," Chris said weakly.

Apparently Roxy felt the same way. "Yes it does. I called Madison and read it to her. She cried like a baby. She agreed with me that the person who could write those words must love me very much."

A proverbial light bulb lit up above Chris's head and his mouth dropped open.

"What are you thinking about?" Roxy asked.

"Oh, nothing, just Cedric."

"What about him?"

"Nothing," Chris said. "We're just so excited to be in the playoffs. That's all."

Roxy apparently didn't want to hear about football. She wrapped her arms around Chris's neck and kissed him again. "I've read that letter over a hundred times and each time it moves me more than the last. Just think of the things you wrote."

Chris was trying to as he flipped through the pages. But he couldn't stop thinking about Cedric. A realization had just landed on him like a ton of bricks. He now knew the truth, a truth that had stared him in the face since the day he and Cedric met, but he was blinded by it. He was so infatuated with Roxy that he couldn't see it. But now it was as clear as the nose on his face. He knew now that he wasn't the only one in love with Roxy.

"Tell me you love me," Roxy said.

"You know I love you."

Roxy smiled. "But the words make all the difference. I always knew words were important, but I never knew they would change my life. When I read that letter, each word feels like your arms wrapped around me. Each syllable is like your lips on mine. Every little thought is like your voice in the darkness that night under my window."

Chris was speechless.

"I have a confession to make though."

Chris looked surprised. "What is it?"

"When I first saw you, I thought you were so handsome. I remember telling Madison how cute you were and how fit you were. I'm ashamed to say I was first attracted to you because of that."

"That's normal. I mean, there's nothing wrong with that."

"But it's not okay," Roxy said. "To want to meet someone just for the outside is childish. I know that now. It would be like wanting to date Anthony for his car."

"Roxy—"

"No, Chris. I'm trying to open up to you here and

bare my soul. I need to do this. I want to apologize for being shallow, for liking you for your looks."

"It's okay," Chris said. Chris was actually used to girls liking him for his looks and he wasn't bothered by that at all. In fact, he knew it was Roxy's looks that drew him to her. "Are you saying you don't find me handsome anymore?"

Roxy laughed. "Yes, but more importantly, I find you beautiful. It is not your looks that made me fall in love with you; it was your soul, your words. I realize now that this handsome face serves a greater purpose, to carry around a beautiful mind. Your appearance wouldn't change that at all. I would think you were the most handsome guy on Earth even if you were ugly."

Chris suddenly spun around to face Roxy. "Do you mean that?"

"Yes."

"You would love me if I were ugly?"

Roxy laughed. "You could never be ugly to me."

"I'm just talking about physically here," Chris clarified. "You would love me no matter how I looked?"

"Yes," Roxy reiterated. "Of course I would."

"What if I were fat?"

Roxy laughed. "I'm sure we both will be some day."

"I'm serious," Chris said with a firm tone. "If I were fat right now, could you still love me?"

"With all my heart," she answered in just as serious a tone.

"Obese?"

"Yes."

Chris searched for more ways to get his point across. "What if I were the fattest guy in the world?"

Roxy's face became dead serious. "Even then I would love you."

Chris stared out the window.

"What is it?" she asked. "Don't you believe me?"

"Of course I do," he said turning back to her. "I just have so much on my mind right now."

"I know you do," she said. "I know you have a lot to think about. I'm not trying to make your life harder. I promise. I just had to let you know how I felt."

Chris leaned over and kissed her gently. "Have you been home to see your parents yet?"

She shook her head.

"Go home then. I have something I have to do. I'll call you later."

Roxy looked confounded but agreed and drove Chris home.

His car was in front of his own house when he got there. Cedric had parked it there and walked home apparently. He got in and drove straight to Cedric's house.

"I haven't seen him since he left for practice," Cedric's mom told Chris at the door.

Chris drove around town looking for him. He tried the Frosty Freeze and other places that Cedric frequented, but no luck. He finally gave up and went home.

That night he tried calling several times but again struck out. He began to wonder if Cedric was avoiding him on purpose. He tried even more over the next few days, but never got him. With Christmas and family visiting, and spending time with Roxy and her family, he was never able to speak with Cedric during the holiday, but he knew he had to.

When school started back after Christmas break, he still hardly saw Cedric since he took none of the advanced math and literature courses that Cedric did. Mostly he just saw him passing in the hall or sitting at lunch, and normally Roxy was by Chris's side or there were simply too many other students around for him to say anything. So he waited.

Many times he saw Anthony also while walking through the halls with Roxy, and he received the same cold-dead stare each time. But that didn't bother him. That he expected. His revelation about Cedric had caught him by surprise and now it was all he could think about.

Finally the day of the first playoff game arrived and he sat beside Cedric during the pep rally in the school gymnasium. But again, it wasn't the proper venue with all the other players around and the crowd yelling and screaming.

Cedric sensed something was going on. "What's up with you?"

"I need to talk to you in private."

Cedric looked around and the entire student body and faculty and shrugged.

Chris nodded and didn't say anything.

He sat with Cedric on the bus ride to the game like he normally did, but neither of them said a word during the entire journey. Several times Chris thought about talking, but didn't want to start something he wasn't sure they would have the time or privacy to finish.

Finally, during the game, Chris spotted his chance. The third quarter was halfway over and they were already leading 35-14. Cedric sat on a bench by himself beside a fan trying to cool off. It was a cold night and other players did not become overheated in this weather, but they weren't Cedric.

"Hey, my friend," Chris said as he sat down beside him.

"Hey, Chris." Cedric returned the greeting.

"Great game, huh?"

Cedric nodded. "I'd say so. You've had a good night."

"Guess what I read last week?" Chris asked, tired of beating around the bush.

"Playboy?"

Chris laughed. "No, I read that last letter you wrote to Roxy when she was visiting her grandmother."

"Oh yeah," Cedric said. "Did you like it?"

"I loved it," Chris said, "but not as much as Roxy. The teardrops were a nice touch. How'd you do that?"

"Just a few drops of water to really sell it, you know."

"Oh yeah." Chris nodded. "Well, it worked. In fact, she told me that only someone who truly loved her could write those words."

Cedric was silent and turned to watch the game.

"I agreed with her," Chris said. "And I feel foolish for not seeing it before."

"What are you talking about?" Cedric asked still looking away.

"You know what I'm saying. You're in love with Roxy. Admit it."

Cedric was silent again.

"And she's in love with you," Chris added.

"What?" Cedric asked spinning to face his friend.

"It's true," Chris said. "She told me she only loves me for my words, my wit, and my knowledge of literature. And that is all you. Why didn't you tell me?"

"I don't know what you're talking about."

"Admit it now or I will tell Roxy myself."

Cedric panicked and grabbed Chris's shoulder pads under his collar. "Say anything and I will beat you to a pulp."

"Do it," Chris said. "Beat me to a pulp. Finish what you wanted to do the first time we met, because that would be better than living a lie. It couldn't hurt any worse. Admit to me you love her or I will walk over to her right now and tell her."

"Okay," Cedric said. "I love her. Are you happy?"

Chris pointed toward Roxy. "Tell her."

"Why are you doing this?"

"Because you're my friend," Chris said. "And because she needs to know the truth so she can decide between us."

"Look at me," Cedric said. "Who could love this? My parents couldn't even love me."

"Roxy said she would love me even if I was fat."

Cedric gasped. "She said that?"

Chris nodded.

"Don't be a jackass," Cedric said. "Look at you. You will never be fat. I know that. You know that. Roxy knows that. Don't put so much stock in what a woman tells you, especially a woman in love. She's doing the same thing to you that we've been doing to her. She's telling you exactly what you want to hear."

"Nice try, my friend," Chris said, "but that's what you're doing to me right now too. I'm not falling for your BS. You have to tell her."

Cedric sighed. "Chris, we did it. Our plan worked. Can't you just be happy that you succeeded?"

Chris shook his head. "How can I be happy knowing my girlfriend is in love with someone else? I love her, but I need her to love me for who I am, not who she thinks I am."

"Nevil."

Chris and Cedric looked up to see the coach.

"Get ready to go in," the coach said and walked away.

Chris got up and put on his helmet. "I'm going to know the truth one way or another."

"Why?" Cedric asked. "Why are you doing this to me?"

"Why shouldn't you be happy?" Chris asked. "You deserve it as much as I do."

Cedric stared at the ground.

"Should I ruin your chance at happiness just because my jeans are thirty inches in the waist?" Chris asked.

Cedric looked up. "Seriously? Thirty?"

Chris smiled.

"Should I ruin your chance at happiness simply because I'm better at using words?" Cedric asked. "Your feelings for Roxy are real, aren't they?"

Chris nodded. "Yes."

"That's all I did," Cedric said. "I just helped you describe them to her. Please don't punish me for that." He looked back to the ground.

Chris was having none of the excuses. "You have until the end of the season to tell her, however long that is."

Cedric looked back up. "What are you saying?"

"I'm saying if we lose tonight, you tell her tonight. If we go all the way to state, you tell her after that game. If you do not, I will tell her. Either way we're going to know who she chooses."

"It will be you," Cedric said.

Chris fastened the chin strap. "I hope so." He turned and jogged away.

Cedric sat there in silence, fear gripping him like never before. He began to regret writing that letter. He looked over at Roxy amongst the other cheerleaders. She was breathtakingly beautiful. His heart ached from simply seeing her. But he knew he couldn't tell her, at least not this night. When he went back into the game, he played like never before, making sure his team won, thus giving him a stay of execution.

CHAPTER FOURTEEN

"It's all come down to this, boys," Cap said as he stared around the circle of teammates in the huddle.

Each player was beat up, bruised, and/or bleeding. It had been a rough game. The starting quarterback had been injured with torn ligaments in the first quarter and the backup quarterback, an inexperienced tenth-grader, was trying to pull off the come-from-behind victory. The score stood 21-17. The Cavaliers were trailing with only ten seconds left to play. The ball rested on the opponents' seventeen yard line.

"The winner of this game goes to state," Cap added, as if anyone wasn't aware of the stakes. "Hey, Cedric, you with us?"

Cedric looked up. His mind was on Roxy. "Yes, I'm with you. Let's do this for Frenchtown, boys."

The young quarterback called the play and everyone cheered and took their position. The rookie nervously stepped behind the center and called for the snap. Everything seemed to happen in slow motion. The defender rushed Cedric and he blocked him successfully, but the linebacker blitzed past Cedric and went for the quarterback. Cedric reached over and was able to grab the bottom of his jersey but he couldn't hold him. The opposing player tore away and was one-on-one with the quarterback. Cedric rushed back but there was nothing he could do. The linebacker zeroed in and made a vicious hit.

But the sophomore was able to throw the ball as the linebacker and another player, a defensive lineman, came crushing down on him.

Cedric stopped and turned to watch the ball in flight. And then he saw him. Chris was breaking for the corner of the end zone, the safety right on his tail.

The ball was overthrown but Chris dove out, his arms reaching out as far as he could, as the ball barely touched his fingertips. But somehow he brought the ball back in and grabbed it firmly as he hit the ground mere inches from the out-of-bounds line deep in the back of the end zone.

The referee threw both hands up to signal a touchdown as the time ran off the clock.

Cedric took off his helmet and cheered loudly. The entire team left the sidelines and ran toward Chris, hoisting him onto their shoulders and carrying him off the field. Chris pointed to Cedric as they passed.

Cedric pointed back as if to say, "You're the man." It wasn't until he saw someone else pointing in the other direction that he realized the quarterback had not gotten up. He rushed to his side. He was conscious but clearly fazed. The coach and team doctor arrived.

The doctor tried asking him questions but the kid didn't seem to understand.

The coach tried snapping his fingers. Nothing.

All cheering stopped as they worked on him. Finally he began to look around as his vision and senses started to return. "I'm okay," he said. "I'm okay."

Cedric wasn't sure about that at all, but he helped the kid up. "You won the game, my friend. You're the hero."

"We won?" the kid asked in wonder.

The coach laughed. "Uh, yeah, let's get you over to the sidelines."

The doctor concurred and Cedric helped him off the field. Everyone cheered but Cedric had a feeling this was not the end of it.

But finally, after an eternity it seemed, the Frenchtown Cavaliers were once again headed to the state championship game.

***

Over the next few days the entire town was abuzz. All the stores had put signs of encouragement in their windows. Some read "Championship Bound." Others read "14-0, One More to Go." The excitement could be felt everywhere you went.

"You guys are doing it. I guess all the talk at the beginning of the season was not just talk."

Cedric smiled across the table at Chris's father. Cedric was eating lunch with them on Sunday, which had pretty much become a tradition. "I guess you're right."

"I'm very proud of you guys," Chris's mom said.

"Thank you, Mrs. Nevil," Cedric said. "I don't think we would be here without Chris's contributions this season."

Chris rolled his eyes as his parents beamed with pride.

"In fact," Cedric continued, "this has been the best year all around for everyone."

"Hear, hear," Mr. Nevil said.

"Really... the perfect year." Cedric stared at Chris. "Almost nothing can take away all we've achieved this year. Almost nothing except maybe self-destruction. But why would anyone in their right mind do anything to tear down this incredible journey? Wouldn't you agree, Chris?"

Chris laughed but his parents were confused.

"Are we missing something, boys?" Chris's dad asked.

Chris nodded. "Always." Then he had a thought. "Hey, guys," he said to his parents, "do you remember what I always wanted to be when I was a little kid?"

His parents searched their memories.

"Oh, I remember," his mom said. "You always wanted to be one of those construction guys who run that one piece of equipment. What was it?"

The dad's eyes lit up and he laughed. "That's right. I remember now too. You always wanted to run one of those wrecking ball vehicles."

"That's right. And guess what," Chris said and looked straight into Cedric's eyes. "I still do."

Cedric laughed. "Touché, my friend."

"What does all that mean?" his mom asked.

Cedric reached his fork across to the dish in the middle of the table. "It means I'll have another one of these incredible pork chops, my dear."

Cedric left Chris's family's house just before dark and walked all the way to the grocery store at the crossing to pick up his mother's medication at the small pharmacy in the back of the aisles. As he neared the parking lot, he noticed two rough-looking guys get out of an old pickup truck and enter the store. It was the t-shirts with cut off sleeves that caught his attention, seeing how it was about thirty-five degrees outside.

As he entered the store he heard someone yell. A woman. A woman who seemed very irritated. He walked over and looked down to the other end of the aisle and saw the two guys standing in front of Roxy. They were taunting her with obscene words and gestures.

"Leave me alone," she screamed.

One of them grabbed her from behind and the other made kissy faces in front of her.

Roxy spit in his face.

Cedric felt the blood filling his cheeks as his temperature rose sharply. He started walking quickly down the aisle, clear on what he was about to do. It was third grade all over again. Before he got there, however, someone else showed up and came to her aid.

"Leave her alone," Anthony Royal shouted.

"Or what?" the guy in front of Roxy asked as he shoved Anthony.

Wrong question. Anthony answered but not with words. He punched him in the face and the man went down hard. The guy lay there on the floor dazed as two streaks of blood, one from each nostril, trailed across his cheeks all the way to the floor.

The other guy let go of Roxy and looked around

at his friend on the floor. That was a mistake as well as Anthony's second punch landed on the back of his head, knocking him on top of his partner.

"Now beat it," Anthony commanded.

They followed his orders this time, got up, and ran out of the store.

"Are you okay?" Cedric asked as he got to Roxy.

"Just a little shaken up," she said. "I'm fine thanks to Anthony."

"I'm not sure you needed me," Anthony said.

Cedric nodded in agreement. "That was some mighty fine spitting."

"Oh no," Roxy said. "Let's not share this story at school."

"Mum's the word," Anthony said and turned to walk away.

"Wait," Cedric called out and walked up to Anthony. "I appreciate what you did."

"What was I supposed to do?" Anthony asked. "Let them pick on a friend of mine?"

Cedric nodded as Anthony once again walked away.

"Wait," Cedric called out and walked up to him again.

"What now? Are you looking for some fighting tips?"

Cedric laughed. "Maybe some other time. You know our starting quarterback is not coming back, right?"

"I heard. I'm sorry about that."

"Well," Cedric continued, "the coach told us today that our backup has a mild concussion and his doctor has recommended he take it easy for a while. That means he won't be able to play Friday night either."

Anthony frowned. "I didn't know that. That's a tough break, what with the championship game Friday night."

"It sure is," Cedric, agreed. "So we don't have a quarterback right now at all."

Anthony looked puzzled as his eyes squinted. "What are you getting at?"

Cedric smiled. "Think you can learn the offense in five days?"

Anthony laughed. "You're kidding, right?" He looked at Roxy who had joined them. "He's kidding, right?"

Roxy and Cedric both shook their heads.

"He sounds very serious to me," Roxy said. "You're a natural. We need someone we can count on."

"No more false flattery please," Anthony said.

"You're right," Cedric said. "I doubt you're smart enough to learn our offense."

Anthony laughed. "I don't know what's more offensive, or juvenile: false flattery or that pathetic attempt at reverse psychology."

Cedric grinned. "Whichever one that works."

He looked right at Cedric for several seconds as if wondering why he was actually considering this. Finally he sighed and shook his head. "Let me run it by my dad and see what he says."

Roxy and Cedric burst out laughing. Anthony thought about what he said and started laughing as well.

The mayor was the biggest fan the team had.

"Okay, I guess I'm in," he said. "But we're not showering together and if I get killed, I'm never speaking to either one of you again."

They all laughed.

***

Cedric, Chris, and Anthony stood outside the team bus. It was still before noon, but the players were to arrive several hours before game time. The sun was hanging lazily over the tree line and there was a brisk nip in the air. It was the big day and the rest of the players were already on board.

Roxy arrived in her car and walked up to them. "I just wanted to say good luck one more time. I wish we could go with you guys, but the cheerleaders will be there in a few hours."

Chris gave her a hug. "Thanks, sweetie."

Roxy stepped back and looked at Anthony. "Nervous?"

He nodded and looked at Chris and Cedric. "Yeah, but we have a lot of talent on this team. None right here in immediate company, but a lot of it on the bus."

Cedric smiled.

"I'm going to board, guys." Anthony went aboard the bus and took a seat.

"I guess we'll see you on the field," Cedric said.

Roxy nodded as Cedric followed Anthony.

"And after the game," Chris said, "Cedric has something to talk to you about."

Roxy looked confused. "Oh? What is it, Cedric?"

Cedric froze in the doorway of the bus. "Uh, nothing important."

"Okay, you guys play your hearts out," she said.

Cedric and Chris boarded the bus and sat with each other. They both waved to Roxy as the bus pulled away. As soon as she was out of sight, Cedric smacked Chris on the back of his head.

Chris laughed. "Making sure you didn't forget."

"How could I?" Cedric was more nervous about the talk than he was the big game. "I can't believe you won't let this go. You're the most stubborn person I have ever met."

"Ha," Chris said. "That's the kettle... uh, the black pot... uh..."

Cedric laughed. "I smacked you too hard. I hope you haven't forgotten how to catch a football."

Two hours later the bus pulled into the parking lot of Neyland Stadium in Nashville where the Cavaliers were to take on the Bulldogs for the Tennessee State High School Championship.

The Bulldogs were also undefeated and had destroyed all of their opponents. Unlike the Cavaliers, every one of their linemen, on offense and defense, were big and strong guys like Cedric, although not as large in the midsection of course. Their quarterback was all-state, the tailback had over 1000 yards for the season, and two of their wide receivers were being scouted by several large colleges. The boys from Frenchtown knew they had their work cut out for them.

An official led the team to their dressing room

so they could store their gear until time to get dressed. Afterward the coach took them out to see the stadium. It was the most incredible sight Cedric had ever seen.

Next came Cedric's favorite part: food. They filtered into a lunch hall and each grabbed a meal prepared by the staff, a steak-like patty with all the trimmings. Cedric, Chris, and Cap sat together.

Cedric looked up and saw Anthony trying to decide where to sit and motioned him over.

Anthony sat across from them. "Thanks." He looked down at his plate. "So, what is this?"

Cedric raised both hands and waved the middle and index fingers to signify quotation marks. "Meat."

"Perfect," Anthony said.

The coach walked over and sat a large pink tablet on the table in front of Cedric. "There you go, champ."

Cedric swallowed the pill with a swig of tea.

"What was that?" Anthony asked.

"Steroids," Cedric answered.

"Don't listen to him,' Chris said. "It's a salt pill because he sweats a ton."

Cedric nodded.

Anthony still hadn't taken the first bite. "Question. Is it normal to be this nervous right now?"

All three nodded.

"It will go away," Cap said, "after you get knocked on your butt the first time."

Cedric and Chris agreed.

"Okay," Anthony said. "That's reassuring." He rubbed his hands on his pants legs. "My hands are sweating like crazy."

"Maybe you need a salt pill," Chris said.

"I got your back," Cedric said. "Hey, Bobby."

The team's center got up from another table and walked over. "What's up, boss?"

"Make sure you keep the towel on today," Cedric said.

"You got it," he said and walked back to his seat.

"What was that about?" Anthony asked.

"He'll have a towel tucked in his pants," Cap answered. "It will hang down behind him for you to wipe your hands on."

Anthony looked impressed. "Alright then. Now let's try this so-called *meat*."

After the meal, going over the plays and strategy, a pep talk, and a prayer, the Frenchtown Cavaliers took the field. Many residents had driven the distance to watch their boys play for the title and the stands were full.

The mayor sat on the front row of the fifty-yard line and cheered his heart out. He now had more reasons to pull for this team.

Cedric glanced over at the cheerleaders and found Roxy. It was a motion that was second nature to him. But this time he quickly looked away so he could concentrate solely on the game.

The time for the coin flip came and Cedric and Cap walked across to meet the captains for the other team. Cap called for heads, won the toss, and chose to defer the kickoff to the second half. The other captains chose with side to defend for the first half.

The game commenced as the Cavaliers kicked the

ball deep. From there it went downhill fast. The defense could not stop the backs or receivers. The Bulldogs took the ball the length of the field and scored on the opening possession.

The extra point was good and the score stood 7-0.

After the kickoff, the offense took the field. Anthony had been to every practice but this would be his first real snap. He looked over at the coach and relayed the call to his teammates in the huddle. It was a pass play.

He squatted behind the center. "Blue 73. Blue 73. Hut."

The center hiked the ball and Anthony drifted back into the pocket. But the defense blitz. A huge linebacker rushed through the line and had a free shot at Anthony, catching him and driving him hard to the ground before he could throw the ball.

The opposing side cheered.

Cedric rushed back to see if he was okay.

Anthony jumped right up, apparently more angry than hurt. No more butterflies. No more anxiety. Now it was war.

"All right," Cedric said. "We got us a quarterback."

Anthony looked to the coach for the next call, but this time signaled to the coach what he thought they should run. The coach gave him a thumb's up and he walked into the huddle. Weary and defeated eyes stared back at him. They looked like the downtrodden of the apocalypse. They were unable to stop this team's offense, and now, after only one play, it appeared they were no match for their defense. Anthony knew he needed to turn this attitude around. "Okay, fellas, look alive. These guys ain't crap. They're no different than any ass wipe you've faced all season. And you know no one's a bigger asshole than I am."

"He's got a point," Cedric said.

Every player in the huddle perked up and several even laughed.

Anthony nodded and continued. "If these idiots like to blitz so much, let them. That means the middle is going to be wide open, so let's run it down their freaking throats."

The spirit and confidence of every guy in that huddle went sky high.

Anthony walked up to the center again. "Red 34. Red 34. Hut. Hut."

This time it was a quick handoff. The linebacker rushed again but blew right past the fullback with the ball as he followed Cedric's block, which drove his guy right to the ground leaving a hole you could have driven a truck through. The runner scrambled for nineteen yards and a first down before the safety could tackle him.

And in that defining moment the Cavaliers knew they could hold their own with this team.

CHAPTER FIFTEEN

"We're only down seven points," the coach said as he paced back and forth in front of his team during half-time. The score was 28-21, so it was still anyone's game. It had been a brutal first half. The Cavaliers had already lost three starters with injuries, nothing serious, but enough to keep them out of the rest of the game. Every player who had been in this game was hurting.

The Bulldogs were faring no better.

"We can win this thing," the coach continued. "We're going to make some changes in the second half. I want Cap, Cedric, and Anthony to play offense and defense. I know you're hurting, Anthony, but you think you can go both ways?"

"He can do it," Cedric said. "He can definitely go both ways."

"Thanks, man," Anthony replied.

"Just ask his boyfriend," Cedric added.

Everyone laughed, including Anthony and the coach. It was a much-needed laugh to break the obvious tension.

"Well, all right," the coach said. "I want someone else to talk now, someone who has a way with words."

Cedric looked up. He didn't feel like giving a pep

talk, but would if the coach thought it would help.

"Anthony," the coach said. "Come on up here."

Anthony looked up. He was as shocked, or more so, as Cedric. He got up, with effort, from the wooden bench that ran in front of the lockers and walked with a slight limp to the front. His ankle was in bad shape. All of his knuckles were bruised. His ribs hurt and his throwing arm was killing him, but he dared not tell the coach.

Many on the team cheered. Like him or not, they knew that Anthony stepping in as quarterback was why they were still in this game and had a shot.

"Coach," Anthony said as he stood where the coach had been. "I don't really know what to say, guys. I'm not a great writer like Cedric. All I can really say is thank you. Thank you for letting me be a part of this. You've all worked hard for the entire season. No matter what happens out there in the second half, you are all winners. No matter what happens, the town will always remember this night. They'll remember each and every one of you and how you gave your all, more than your all, to bring this title home. They will stand behind us no matter what. They will care about this team for the rest of our lives whether we win or lose. If they love us that much, I guess the question we each need to ask ourselves is this: how much do we love them? Do we want to give them a second place finish?" Anthony's voice rose high and loud for his next and last line. "Or do we want to give them everything?"

All the players jumped to their feet and screamed and cheered so loudly the walls shook.

At that moment, Cedric was actually proud of Anthony.

And that was what the coach was looking for; the mental boost to get the adrenaline flowing. "All right, men; let's win this thing."

Players from both teams gave their all as the lead changed sides throughout the entire second half. With only twenty-two seconds remaining, the Cavaliers called their last time out. It was fourth down and they were down 42-35 and on the Bulldogs' six yard line, six yards away from tying the game and going into overtime.

"You make the call, Anthony," the coach said as they huddled around him.

The Cavaliers took the field for the last seconds of a miracle season.

Anthony stared around the circle. Every player was tired and hurting, especially Cedric. Playing offense and defense was hard enough for Cap and Anthony, but Cedric was absolutely exhausted. They had started double-teaming and triple-teaming him right from the kick-off of the second half to shut down the run. Anthony had to start passing more to keep the ball moving.

"We're this close, guys. I think they are expecting us to pass, so we're going to fool them. We're going to run a draw play." Anthony nodded to the small second-string running back. "The linemen are going to pass block, the receivers are going for the corners, and that will make their linebackers drift back."

The little running back swallowed hard.

"You can do this. You just run right toward this guy," Anthony said nodding toward Cedric, "and Cedric the Bulge will clear you a path all the way to the end zone."

Every player in the huddle froze. Had they heard Anthony right? Had he said what they just thought he said? All eyes turned to Cedric afraid of what was about to happen.

Cedric stared right at Anthony then looked at the rest of them, their tired and bloodshot eyes longing for a sign, a hint of belief, of comradery, of anything. Cedric stuck his hand in the middle of the group with his palm facing down and said, "You damn right. Let's do this."

They all laid their hands on top of Cedric's and yelled as they broke the huddle and took their places at the line of scrimmage. Eleven individuals pushed to their mechanical limits and beyond. Eleven individuals with one goal.

Anthony limped noticeably up to the center and crouched down. "Green 19. Green 19. Hut." He took the snap and drifted back in the pocket, holding the ball up beside his head as if to pass.

The receivers ran wide with their hands in the air. The linemen stood and blocked like it was going to be a pass. It worked. The defensive linebackers drifted back deep into the end zone to try to knock the ball down or intercept it. Instead Anthony handed the ball to the tailback. Cedric dropped his head and started driving his opponent backward. He drove him all the way into the end zone and kept driving until he heard the whistle blow.

The first thing he saw when he looked around was the refs raising their arms high in the air. Then he looked down and saw that little running back lying at his feet clutching the ball with all his might. Cedric reached down and lifted him completely over his head as all his teammates cheered and the fans in the stands jumped up and down.

Cedric jogged off the field in a state of euphoria. He was so caught up in the game, he had completely forgotten about Roxy and having the talk. All he knew at this moment was that his team was only an extra point kick away from overtime. He went straight to the bench to sit and rest.

Chris came over with a cup of sports drink and handed it to Cedric. "That was incredible."

Cedric nodded and drank the entire cupful in one gulp. Then he noticed the people on the field. "What's going on?"

"They have an injured man," Chris said. "I think it was your man. They say you knocked him silly and they're afraid to move him right now. It could be a while."

"Great game, guys."

They looked up to see Roxy and both greeted her.

"I need to speak with the coach," Chris said. "We have a moment, so this would be a good time for you guys to talk." At that he hopped up off the bench and walked away.

Roxy sat beside Cedric. "Okay. What is this mysterious thing you need to tell me?"

Cedric stared in the direction where Chris went and could not believe what he had just done. He looked back to Roxy. "Uh… Roxy, Chris just wanted me to talk to you."

"About what?"

His breathing escalated. "I don't know how to begin."

"I think I know what this is about," Roxy said.

"You do?"

She nodded. "I'm not sure he believed what I told him when I came back from my grandmother's. He's been acting weird ever since."

"What did you tell him?" Cedric asked even though he knew the answer.

"I told him it was his soul I loved," Roxy explained. "I told him it was his words and not his looks that made me love him."

"Is that true?"

Roxy smiled. "Of course it is."

Cedric stared right into Roxy's eyes. "So then is it also true that you told him you would love him even if he were ugly?"

"Yes, it's true. I would love him if he were ugly or even if he were…" Roxy suddenly stopped and dropped her eyes.

"What?" Cedric asked. "Fat? Is that it? You can say the word. I won't be offended."

"Yes," Roxy said looking up again, "even fat."

"Obese?" Cedric asked.

"Yes."

Cedric breathed a sigh of relief. It was one thing to hear Chris say it, yet another to hear it come directly from the source. "Oh, Roxy, I want to tell you something but for the first time in my life I'm at a loss for words. Roxy, I—"

The crowd behind them cheered loudly.

"What is it?" Roxy asked.

"We just tied the game."

While they were talking, the injured player had run off the field under his own power and the Cavaliers' special teams had made the extra point kick.

Cedric looked at the timeclock. Sixteen seconds remaining. The kickoff unit took the field.

He looked back at Roxy. "We have a little more time now. Once the clock runs out, we'll have a short break before overtime."

"Then tell me what is it you're trying to tell me," she said.

The kickoff took off down field, a low kick to help prevent a runback.

"I want you to know..." Cedric tried hard.

"Yes."

"I need you to know—"

"Fumble!" the crowd shouted.

Cedric jumped up and looked to see a pile of players from each team on the Bulldogs' forty-yard line. He watched as the refs pulled the players away like sardines. When they got to the bottom, two of the refs pointed toward the Bulldogs' end zone to signal the Cavaliers had recovered the fumble.

The Frenchtown crowd erupted.

"Offense!" the coach yelled.

"I have to go, Roxy. We'll talk later." Cedric rushed onto the field putting his helmet on as he ran.

Roxy went back to the cheerleaders.

"We caught a break, boys," Anthony said in the

huddle. "We've practiced this play, the Hail Mary. All backs and receivers run to the end zone. No one stays in to block. I'll throw it as hard as I can."

Cedric walked up to the line. He cleared his mind of Roxy and looked at the guy in front of him, a new guy, a smaller backup lineman. The kid looked up at Cedric and swallowed hard. Cedric got into his stance and placed his right hand on the ground, his fingers outstretched with white knuckles from where the blood rushed away. Sweat dripped from his brow.

The ball was snapped and Cedric blocked his guy hard, so hard he fell back on the ground. Cedric looked around and saw Anthony backing up. He quickly moved in front of him to offer more protection. One defensive end and one tackle broke free, followed close behind by one of the linebackers. Cedric planted his feet and took them on.

Then something happened that had never happened before. His knees buckled and he went down. The three defenders plowed right over him and made a beeline for the quarterback.

Anthony pulled back and threw the ball with all his might just before the three ran him over in the same fashion. But the ball was away.

Cedric still lay on the ground but propped himself up with his right arm to watch.

Anthony lay right beside him and also propped himself up to watch.

Four Bulldogs grouped together in the end zone to await the pass. Two Cavaliers stood with them. All six had their hands raised as high as they could.

Then Cedric saw him. Chris was running straight down the middle of the field, right toward the mob. At the last second he leapt into the air, higher than a human being should be able to. Cedric saw the ball land in his hands. But that's the last he could see of him from his position.

Chris hit the other player in full stride, his fingers curling as tight as they could around the leather ball. Then he tumbled over several players, his feet straight up in the air as he came down on his head, the entire mob diving on top of him.

Cedric looked to the stands for a clue as to what happened. The hometown crowd was on their feet but not cheering. He looked at the opposite side. The Bulldog fans were on their feet too, but they weren't cheering either. Cedric jumped to his feet and ran toward the end zone. He saw the coach running too. He saw the coach from the other side running too. He saw the doctor running. And he saw Roxy running.

When he got there, the players had moved away and the refs were waving frantically. There lay Chris gripping the ball firmly in his right arm. There lay Chris after making the winning touchdown completion. There lay Chris, the hero of the night. There lay Chris, his friend. There lay Chris completely motionless.

He spun around and saw Roxy running as fast as she could and he caught her in his huge arms.

"Let me go," she screamed. "Let me get to him."

As hard as it was to restrain her, Cedric knew it was more important for the medical team to do their job, so he held fast.

Roxy buried her head into his jersey and cried.

A paramedic quickly called for an ambulance and one drove right onto the field. Chris was placed on a stretcher and loaded inside and it drove away.

"Take me to him, Cedric," Roxy pleaded. "Please take me."

"I will. I promise." Cedric looked up and saw Roger. "Hold onto her until I can get a ride."

Roger put his arms around Roxy and tried to comfort her.

Cedric ran to the dressing room and began to change without even showering.

"They're taking him to Nashville General."

Cedric looked up to see the coach. Then he saw Anthony. "Can your dad take us?"

Anthony nodded then ran out to find his dad.

Cedric left the dressing room and looked for Roger and Roxy, but they were no longer on the field. He followed the entrance to the outside. People were everywhere. He looked around and saw Anthony coming, still in his uniform.

"My dad's coming," he said as he ran up. "Where's Roxy?"

"I don't know. She was with Roger."

Anthony looked around. There was plenty of light, but also plenty of people.

A man walked up to them as they scanned around the panoramic view. He wore a long sleeve white shirt with the sleeves rolled up and a brown tie loosely fixed around his neck.

"Hello, Cedric," he said as he walked up. "Do you

have a minute?"

Cedric shook his head. "No, I'm sorry, I do not."

"We have to get to the hospital," Anthony said.

"I understand," the man replied. "But here's my card." He handed Cedric a business card.

"What is this?" Cedric asked.

"I'm with the Volunteers," the man answered. "Call me next week. I want to offer you a full scholarship to play football for us next year."

The man walked away as Anthony stared in disbelief. Then he saw them. "Roger! Roxy!"

Roger and Roxy walked over at the same time as the mayor showed up.

"Let's go," the mayor said.

Roger said goodbye as the mayor, Anthony, Cedric, and Roxy walked to his car. They got in and the mayor drove to the hospital.

No one spoke as they drove. The only sound inside the car was Roxy sniffling. Anthony wanted to tell everyone about Cedric's good fortune, but he knew it wasn't the time.

They arrived at the hospital and the mayor let them off at the emergency room entrance and went to park.

"We're here about Chris Nevil," Anthony told the lady at the desk.

She checked her computer and directed them to the third floor trauma ward.

The mayor walked in and joined them as they went to the elevators.

They found the waiting room and Chris's parents

were already there. Roxy ran to them and they put their arms around her. The dad looked up at Cedric. "We don't know anything yet. He's in emergency surgery is all we know."

Anthony had removed his shoulder pads, which just left a grey undershirt. It was stained with sweat and blood. He sat by his dad. Everyone had taken a seat but Cedric. He stood on the other end of the waiting room and paced back and forth for what seemed like an hour.

Finally a doctor came in and everyone gathered around him, all except Cedric who stayed on the far end of the room. He couldn't hear what was being said, nor did he need to. When Chris's mom put her hands over her mouth and Roxy dropped to her knees and cried uncontrollably, Cedric knew.

He followed behind as they were led to the room where Chris lay. The machine that monitors the heartbeat, heartrate, and blood pressure was turned off. Cedric stared at his friend. He looked peaceful. He looked like he was sleeping. But he wasn't; he was gone forever. He was dead. And so was Cedric.

He couldn't bear to watch and turned and walked back to the waiting room. "My best friend is dead," he whispered. "And the only woman I have ever loved cries for me but doesn't even know it." He took a deep breath and leaned over with his face in his hands. "And she will never know."

CHAPTER SIXTEEN

"I brought you another Diet Coke, Mr. Deburr." The petite girl set the glass filled with ice and soda on the table and picked up the empty glass.

"Thank you, Misty," Cedric said. "I see your dad is working you hard."

"Yes, always," Misty Sims replied and shot a glare at her father, Roger, who stood a mere ten feet away behind the counter with the register.

The afternoon sun shone brightly through the windows of the Frosty Freeze. It was a beautiful fall day. The lunch crowd had come and gone and Cedric made up the only customer.

The place looked the same as it always had. The walls had been painted within the last few years, but the tables and chairs were the same ones that had been there since it opened. The menus were upgraded with fancier graphics, but the items listed on them had not changed either, nor the way they were prepared or the equipment used to prepare them,

Roger's parents had retired and moved to Florida and he now ran the Frosty Freeze with his wife, Madison, the former cheerleader at Frenchtown High School, and his youngest daughter. His two older daughters were currently attending college at the University of Tennessee. Roger had gotten a little heavier and his once thinning blond hair was now scattered gray strands. But he was still one of Cedric's oldest, dearest, and very few true friends.

"Can you talk to him?" Misty pleaded. "And tell him I should have Friday nights and Saturday nights off?"

Cedric laughed. "I'll see what I can do."

Misty smiled and walked away.

Cedric returned his focus to the laptop in front of him. This was his favorite place to come write his articles for the newspaper. He still lived in the small house where he grew up and was still as large as ever. He also still walked everywhere he went although he had a license and could drive. No one knew why he did that given that he could no longer walk very well. The years of football had taken their toll and his wooden walking cane hung over the chair beside him.

He stared at his reflection in the screen. He seemed older than his years. His short sideburns were salt-and-pepper and the bags under his eyes could have been manufactured by Samsonite.

It had been twenty-eight years since they captured the state championship, but it felt to him another lifetime. And it wasn't the aching joints that sometimes woke him in agony in the middle of the nights that were his most frequented demons. It wasn't the thoughts of what might have been that continually wreaked havoc on his conscience. It was the nights between sleep and consciousness where he would see Chris leaping for that football and not being able to stop him. That was the image that haunted him relentlessly. Sometimes he stared into nothingness for hours.

Roger came over and sat with Cedric.

Cedric stopped typing to look up at his old classmate. "When are you going to write another play, my friend?"

Roger chuckled. "I think my writing days are over."

"Oh, don't say that. What about poetry?"

Roger shook his head. "I just live vicariously through you now."

Cedric laughed loudly. "I had no idea your life was so sad and pathetic."

"Now you know." Roger shook his head. "That's life as we get older I guess. You should come to one of the class reunions and see how sad and pathetic life really is."

"I guess I should." But Cedric knew he never would. He wasn't that close with a lot of those people when he was in school.

Roger patted his belly. "You'll see we're all trying to catch up with you."

Cedric faked a frown and held up his fist.

Roger held his hands up in surrender. He knew that one topic was still taboo. He returned to the counter.

Three young football players from Frenchtown High, one senior and two freshmen, walked into the restaurant, each wearing letterman jackets, which displayed the large blue F on the fronts. They sat at another table and Misty waited on them. She knew them all.

After she took their orders and walked away, Cedric could hear them whispering.

"That's him," one of them said.

"Are you sure?"

Cedric grimaced.

Finally the three boys walked over and stood in front of his table.

"Mr. Deburr," the senior said. "I'm glad you're here. Can you tell these two freshman newbies the story?"

Cedric smiled and shook his head. "You've heard it enough; you should be able to tell it yourself."

"You were really on the championship team?" one of the younger lads asked.

"I told you he was," the senior barked. He turned and pointed to the huge framed picture mounted on the wall behind Cedric. "That's the team right there."

"Which one are you?" the other freshman asked.

Cedric and Roger both burst out laughing. Cedric took his cane and pushed himself up from his seat. His lower back was stiff from sitting so long. His knees ached and popped as he rose. He turned and walked slowly over to the picture. He took his cane and pointed to himself sitting right on the front row, dead center, looking twice as large as the other players.

"That's me right there," he said tapping the end of his cane to his image. "I'm the skinny fellow in the middle." Cedric continued to stare at the picture, especially at the player to his right, Chris Nevil. Then he looked over at the small square picture of Anthony Royal, which had been added later since the picture was taken at the beginning of the season when Anthony was not yet part of the team.

"Will you tell us the story?" the senior asked again.

"Very well," Cedric said, not only because the boy asked politely but because he really did love telling it.

Roger came out from behind the counter and sat at Cedric's table. He loved hearing it too even though he had heard Cedric tell it several times a year since it happened.

Cedric's eyes glistened and took on a distant look as he recounted the events. "It was twenty-eight years ago and we finished the regular season 11-0. We headed to the state playoffs and our opponents fell one, two, three before us. Then came the championship game against the mighty Bulldogs. It was a true David versus Goliath scenario. Their linemen were giants like the Nephilim of Biblical lore. Their backs and receivers as fast as the Greek god Mercury. Their quarterback sought after by every college in the country.

"Trying to block them was like running into a brick wall. Trying to catch them was like trying to catch the wind. We were outmatched and it first appeared as if we didn't even belong on the same playing field as those guys. They were that good, and they were that mean.

"One-by-one our teammates fell and had to be carried off the field. But we refused to quit. We refused to go gentle into that good night. Bloodied and bruised we kept going to the line of scrimmage to give it our all.

"'Who are these guys who love punishment?' a Bulldog yelled. 'Why won't they stop?' another cried out.

They had won every game easily until this point, but they soon found out we were armed with a weapon beyond our helmets and pads, a weapon more dangerous than they could have ever anticipated: hope.

"Finally, with the score tied and seconds to go, the Bulldogs made their first and fatal mistake: a fumble. We recovered and had time for one Hail Mary pass. Our new quarterback, with zero experience before this game, faded back and threw the ball just as the entire defensive line came crushing down on him. But what a pass it was, a thing of beauty. Seventy yards through the air it flew like a guided missile.

"Then from out of nowhere he came, the hero of the night, our best receiver. He ran toward the gauntlet with reckless abandon. The gods must have touched him because as tired as he was, he somehow leapt into the air higher than any mortal before or since, and stole the ball away from the outreached hands of every defensive back awaiting its decent.

"When he did a cartwheel in midair, he held onto that ball. When he was piled on by half of both teams, he held onto that ball. Even when the very breath of life was knocked from his body, he held onto that ball.

"The clock ran out as the refs raised their hands. The victory was ours."

"Yes!" the senior yelled.

"Wow!" was all the two freshmen could muster, their eyes as wide open as possible.

"Awesome. You have lived the best life, Mr. De-burr. We would give anything to have been part of that game. Our team has no hope for a playoff spot. We have no talent this year. I don't understand why you didn't go to college and then pro. You could have played for the Titans or Falcons."

Cedric used his cane to lower himself back into his chair. "The best life?" He shook his head. "My friend, I have just realized that we are both idiots. But do not worry; the bulk of the idiocy rests with me. I am the bigger idiot and not just literally for I am old with no excuses. We did not win because we had talent. We won because we had heart. College and pro teams want talent. I could never have played on that level. What's more, surely you must realize that my story is heavily exaggerated. Don't believe everything you hear, guys."

The three young players seemed a little saddened, perhaps because they had upset him.

"Thanks for the story, Mr. DeBurr," the senior said. "It's still the greatest story ever."

The young men retook their original seats.

Cedric returned his attention to the laptop on the table in front of him.

"He's right. It's still a great story," Roger said. "And you tell it so well."

Cedric smiled.

Roger got up and again walked back behind the counter. Roger did love the story, but he knew the biggest falsehood was that Cedric could not have done more with his football career. He knew of the offer of a full scholarship to play for Tennessee and who knows what could have happened after that? Who knows how differently Cedric's life might have been, then and now? Only Roger and two others, Cap and Anthony, knew about the scholarship and knew the real reason Cedric had not taken the offer — Roxy.

After Chris's death, Roxy became withdrawn and barely finished high school. She never went to college and continued living with her parents and then just her mother until her mother's death a few years ago. Although still an attractive woman, Roxy had lost all interest in material things. The gray roots in her hair went unattended. She was almost a recluse who wore old dresses and hardly left the house unless she was out of cat food. To the younger people of the town she was the quintessential crazy cat-lady and had accumulated over a dozen felines. Friends had long stopped trying to visit, everyone but Cedric, who still went by every Saturday to take her groceries and share any juicy stories of the town. After all, Cedric wrote for the local paper and had privy to all the best gossip.

Cedric stared out the windows. This was what made writing so tough for him, the memories of the past that stole his attention from the present. He had wanted to write the great American novel but found he couldn't commit to such a vigorous demand. He still read a lot, but mostly his favorites, which he had read many times. He first started writing for the newspaper when Anthony's dad still owned it and continued to write even when Anthony briefly took it over. It provided the perfect outlet, one he so desperately needed. But it paid very little and he could barely afford to get by most months.

He tried to shake the old cobwebs from his mind, turned back to the computer, and continued typing. He buckled down and typed for fifteen straight minutes. He definitely wanted to be gone before the dinner crowd arrived. He still became uncomfortable with a lot of people around. He still feared someone might say something about his size, someone who didn't know him for example. And he still feared what he might do in response.

"There we go." Cedric closed the laptop, got up, and headed for the door.

"You finished your article?" Roger asked.

Cedric nodded.

"Let me guess, another story poking fun at a local politician?"

Cedric chuckled and nodded again.

"Can't you write cute stories?" Roger asked. "You know: friendly human interest stories like dog rescues, old ladies who knit sweaters, or a nice story about a friend who runs a restaurant. Why must you ruffle feathers?"

"Feathers are meant to be ruffled, my friend," Cedric said. "Besides, I've already had to give up ice cream. Don't make me give up everything fun."

"Fun can get expensive," Roger said.

Cedric smiled. He knew his friend was right and patted him on the shoulder. "True, but old habits die hard."

***

Anthony Royal sat behind his desk at City Hall and read over some reports. He had been elected mayor twice now as he walked in his dad's footsteps. After graduating college at Duke, he lived in New York, just outside NYC for several years. But after his father died he moved back, sold the newspaper, and bought the local country club. His time was spent pretty evenly between there, City Hall, and with his wife and teenage son.

His office wall was adorned with the same championship picture that hung in the Frosty Freeze, only with a more expensive frame, and some days he spent hours staring at it. It hung beside his diploma.

"Mr. Mayor."

Anthony looked up to see his assistant sticking her head in the door.

"They're ready for you."

Anthony nodded, grabbed a folder from his desk, and walked to the conference room. This was his least favorite part of the job, but he positioned himself at the head of the table and looked out at the six councilmembers along the sides, three men and three women.

He called the meeting to order and they went over old business, financials, and then he called for new business.

One of the women spoke up. "Once again this year the holiday committee is asking you to be the Grand Marshall of the Thanksgiving Parade."

Anthony rolled his eyes.

"I think it's a great idea," one of the men said. "Not just because you're the mayor, but because of the title you brought home. You're a hero."

All the others nodded.

"I agree," one of the other women said. "You have to understand that it's the most incredible thing that most citizens of this town ever experienced. And people around these parts never forget. That's how much it meant to everyone."

Everyone other than Anthony was in agreement.

The mayor nodded slowly before speaking. "In that case, I think they should ask Ralph Klines to be the Grand Marshall."

All six council members looked around at each other, that look you have when you wonder if you're the only one completely in the dark.

The mayor continued. "He's still living in town. In fact, he and his wife own a small insurance company. They have an office over on 2nd Street."

The confused expressions continued. Finally one of the women asked the obvious.

"Who's Ralph Klines?"

Anthony looked at each member as if he couldn't believe they were asking. "He's the reason we won the championship."

Silence.

"He was the quarterback in the game before the final game. He threw the game-winning touchdown in the final seconds and suffered a concussion on the play. Had it not been for that, he would have led the team to victory against the Bulldogs."

"Well, uh…," the councilwoman said stammering, "I could suggest that to the holiday committee I guess."

"Okay then," Anthony said, "I guess we're through here." With that he adjourned the meeting, got up and went back to his office followed by two of the male members of the council. They always wanted a few minutes in private after each meeting, so he motioned for them to come in.

They sat in the two wingback chairs in front of him and one tossed today's newspaper onto his desk.

"He's gone too far this time," he snapped.

Anthony calmly picked up the paper and read the headline, "Frenchtown City Hall: Corruption or Incompetence?" He smiled as he read Cedric's name underneath the title. "It's just satire, gentlemen. Learn to laugh at yourself and you'll be a lot happier."

"How can this not bother you?' the other councilman asked.

Anthony didn't reply. He didn't think the question warranted validation.

"Someone needs to teach that guy a lesson."

Anthony laughed. "And who will be the teacher? You, professor? He might be getting old, but his fists still pack a wallop."

"Who said anything about fighting?" the councilman asked. "People have accidents all the time. Could happen to anyone. Sometimes they just slip on banana peels."

"If that's all you guys have to do, you can excuse yourselves," Anthony said. "I have actual work to do."

He tried to go back to reading reports after the guys left, but he couldn't get the words out of his head. He wondered if that was a real threat he had just heard. He decided to get out of the office.

He walked to his car and planned to drive to the country club, but that even seemed pointless this day, so

CHAPTER SEVENTEEN

Anthony drove his new Mercedes down the long drive-way to his very large brick house that he and his wife had built when they moved to Frenchtown.

"Well, this is a surprise," his wife said as he walked into the house much earlier than normal.

Anthony couldn't even muster up a smile.

"That bad?" she asked.

He laughed. "Just crazy stuff. I warned you about how exciting life would be in a small town."

His wife nodded. "Yes, you did. But you didn't tell me you were going to run for mayor and be knee-deep in it."

Anthony smiled and nodded. He hadn't planned on being mayor but when pushed by several town offi-cials to run, he threw his hat in the ring.

His wife came from a well-to-do family as well. She was a beautiful woman with dark brown hair and an athletic figure. Even at forty-six years of age, she did aerobics several times a week and jogged every morning. They had met in New York City eighteen years earlier, fell in love, and married.

Their son, Marcus, was fifteen years old and loved computers and gaming, but had no interest in sports.

Anthony was fine with that. He was not like his father in that regard. In fact, had his son taken an interest in football, he might have tried to discourage it.

"I was about to go grocery shopping," his wife said. "Want to come with me?"

"Sure. That actually sounds like it will be the highlight of my day."

Anthony drove them to the grocery store, the same one where he had defended Roxy so many years before. They grabbed a shopping cart and he pushed it as his wife picked out items. Several people recognized the mayor and spoke as they passed.

When they turned down the aisle where pet food was located, there she was. Even though they lived in the same town, he hadn't seen Roxy since he moved back home. Suddenly those old feelings came rushing back, feelings he thought were dead and buried.

She didn't notice him.

He walked past but decided it would be rude not to speak. He turned back. "Hello, Roxy."

Roxy looked up but it took her a few seconds to know who it was. "Oh my gosh. Anthony." She hugged him. "Or should I say 'your honor'? How have you been?"

"Great," Anthony said. "Uh, this is my wife, Jennifer."

Jennifer gave Roxy a hug. "Nice to meet you. I've heard so much about you."

"Really?"

Jennifer nodded. "Well, not just from Anthony, but I've heard several people mention you at the class reunions."

"Good things I hope."

Jennifer smiled and nodded.

"Well it's nice to meet you too, Jennifer. Did your husband ever tell you he saved my life right here in this store?"

Jennifer was surprised and looked at Anthony. "No, he has not."

Anthony shook his head. "That's a bit of an exaggeration I assure you. At most I saved her some embarrassment."

"Don't listen to him," Roxy said. "He's being modest. Two guys were attacking me and he rode in like a knight in shining armor."

Jennifer looked at her husband in dismay. "Really?"

Anthony simply shook his head.

Roxy nodded. "First he rescued me then he rescued the football team."

Anthony's wife rolled her eyes. "That story I know all too well."

The mayor smiled and nodded.

After a few seconds of awkward silence, Jennifer excused herself. "I'm going to keep shopping. You guys catch up." She took the cart and went on ahead.

After she disappeared around the end of the aisle, Anthony looked back at Roxy. "It's really good to see you again."

"And you as well. You're looking good and your wife is very pretty."

"Thanks," Anthony said. "I can't believe you never got married. Did you just never meet the right person?"

Roxy smiled. "Yes, I did. You met him too. His name was Chris and he played football with you. Remember?"

"That was a long time ago, Roxy. Why haven't you moved on?"

She shook her head. "If you had known him the way I did, you wouldn't have to ask."

"I'm very sorry."

"I appreciate it," she said. "But really, I'm content. I have pictures, my memories, and all his letters saved."

Anthony lowered his head but nodded. Then he looked back up. "Tell me, do you ever see Cedric?"

A huge smile crept across Roxy's face. "Every Saturday. He comes by and reads his columns to me, tells me silly jokes, and complains relentlessly about my cats and my paintings."

"His writings have upset a lot of people."

"But it's just comedy," Roxy said. "Surely people understand that. Besides, nobody would ever cross Cedric. He's still as mean as ever."

Anthony laughed. "I'm sure he is. You know, back in school I couldn't stand him."

Roxy laughed. She knew that was true.

"But now," Anthony added, "I think we could be friends."

"You and he friends?" Roxy asked.

"I know. We don't exactly run in the same circles. I have a great family and he has no one. But still, I envy him at times and I think I would enjoy seeing him again."

"I think he would enjoy that too," Roxy added. "He could use a few more friends. I worry about him so. But it's not just him being alone that bothers me. He doesn't take care of himself like he should, and he barely gets by it seems. Sometimes I wish I could buy him a new coat. I think he's been wearing the same one for many winters."

Anthony smiled. "That's not too unusual. I'd give a dollar if I could get my son to change his t-shirt more than once a week."

Roxy laughed.

"You don't have to worry about Cedric," Anthony said. "He's stronger than we know. In fact, he might be the strongest man I've ever known, and I don't mean just physically. Not to mention stubborn as a mule."

Roxy nodded in agreement.

"He lives life on his terms," Anthony continued. "Believe me when I say not all of us have that luxury."

Roxy smiled. "You appear to be doing quite well, Mr. Mayor."

"Oh, I know. It looks on the surface like everything in my life worked out the way it was supposed to. And I guess it did. But it feels also like it was laid out before me without my input or control. I'm not complaining and it's not really regret; it just feels like the more success one achieves, the more freedom they sacrifice. Sometimes I wish I could trade places with Cedric, if even just for a little while."

"That's a very nice thing to say."

"Well, it was good to see you again," Anthony said.

"Yes, you as well."

Anthony started to walk away but stopped and turned back. "While it's true what you said about no one wanting to fight Cedric, this morning in my office two councilmen were complaining about his articles. One of them said something that gave me pause. It was probably just false bravado, but who knows? When you see Cedric Saturday, tell him to keep his eyes open and his wits about him."

"Thank you, Anthony. I will." All expressions of happiness left her face.

He nodded and walked away.

***

Cedric sipped his Diet Coke and looked at the clock. It was 7:30 on a Friday night and he had stopped in the Frosty Freeze to see Roger. Several people sat at other tables and dined. He didn't usually come out this late, but sometimes his small empty house became too small and it felt like the walls were closing in and he couldn't breathe.

Seeing a hulking silhouette moving slowly beside the roads had become a familiar sight for the drivers in Frenchtown.

Cedric sighed. Sometimes he wasn't comfortable anywhere and it wasn't physical. Sometimes he dreaded going home, and every night he dreaded trying to fall asleep. But this night he actually had somewhere to go, so he rose and headed to the front door.

"Leaving so soon, Cedric?" Roger asked. "Why

don't you stay and have supper with me? I can make us something here and we can go to my house and eat."

"Where is Madison tonight?" Cedric asked.

"Getting her hair and nails done… for the third time this week."

Cedric laughed. "I'll take a raincheck, my friend. My editor at the paper is treating me to a real meal tonight."

Roger grinned. "Sounds good. Well, anytime you want a fake meal, we're here for you."

Cedric smiled and nodded. Then he saw the stack of publications on the counter. "Ah, the latest trash rag is out, I see. I can't believe you allow this garbage in your place."

A new publication had started up a year earlier in Frenchtown and the surrounding areas. It was titled *Oui Town* and Cedric despised it. Most of the articles were written by someone who simply used his first name or perhaps a fake name: Horace. It was believed he owned the publication, but no one knew for sure. It was not uncommon these days for someone to say, "Do you know what Horace said?" Cedric hated that sentence and the person. Not only did they print trashy headlines, they also stole stories from the *Frenchtown Gazette*, the paper Cedric wrote for.

"Have you read it this week?" Roger asked.

"You know I never read it."

"Well…" Roger hesitated.

"What is it?"

Roger took a deep breath. "Horace stole part of a story from you, word-for-word. You remember the article you wrote years ago about the Bible belt blues? That's the one, the part about the connection to church and football. He even put his own name on it like he wrote it."

Cedric chuckled. "Have people commented on it?"

Roger nodded. "Everyone loved it. I've heard some say it's the funniest thing they've ever read. But he stole it from you and that bothers me."

Cedric nodded. "Horace is smart. Chris was slim and handsome. That's the story of my life. Have a good night, my friend."

Cedric exited the building and walked toward the road.

A man smoking a cigarette stood in the dim light on the side of the building.

"Hey, fatso," the man yelled.

Cedric looked up in disbelief.

"Yes, you, Cedric the Bulge. Your writing stinks."

"You're going to pay for that," Cedric said and, using his cane, walked as fast as he could toward the guy.

But the guy walked away to the back of the building.

Cedric followed.

Once Cedric got back to the delivery area, the guy ran beside a parked car.

"Come back here," Cedric shouted and kept walking after the man.

As he neared the vehicle, however, he realized too late that it was running and someone was sitting in the driver's seat. Suddenly the car leapt forward and rammed

Cedric. He went down hard and didn't move.

***

White.

Cedric blinked.

Still white was all he saw.

As objects came into focus, he saw the chair beside the bed first. Then he heard the beeping sound emanating from the monitor beside the bed. He recognized the room, or at least the layout of the room. He was in Frenchtown General, the small hospital near the high school and the only hospital in town. He had sat in a room just like this all night when his mother passed away.

He could hear conversation and recognized the voices. He couldn't see them but he knew Cap and Roger were right outside his door. He cocked his head to make out the words.

"What are the doctors saying?" Cap asked.

"Just that it's bad," Roger answered. "I shudder to think how bad it would be if Misty hadn't found him behind the restaurant."

"Here comes the doctor," Cap said.

Several seconds of silence passed. Cedric kept motionless to listen.

"What's the word, doc?" Roger asked.

The doctor took a deep breath. "No sense in trying to sugarcoat it. It's very bad. He has several broken ribs and a serious concussion. But the worst thing is the internal bleeding. We can't even tell how many places there are or how bad it is. All we can do is make sure he gets enough blood and keep an eye on him. The first few days are going to be the test. Whatever you do, don't excite him or allow him to try to get up. He has to rest."

Only then did Cedric notice that one of the lines running to his arm was red. He followed the line up to the bag of blood hanging beside the saline solution. It read "O Positive."

"Shhh," Roger said. "I think he's awake."

Roger and Cap walked back in but Cedric pretended to be asleep.

"I'll check back in later," the doctor said.

Roger and Cap thanked the doctor and sat beside Cedric's bed.

After several minutes, Cedric acted as if he just woke. "Hey, guys. What happened?"

"They think you got hit by a car," Roger said.

"Feels like it," Cedric said. "What are the doctors saying?"

Cap took this one. "Just that you need to rest for a few days."

"How long have I been out?"

"A few hours," Roger answered. "It's almost midnight."

Cedric nodded. "Why don't you guys go on home to your families? I'll be fine tonight."

"I'm staying tonight," Cap said. "My wife is visiting her mother for a few days, so I'm good. I'm sure the cafeteria food here is better than anything I can microwave anyway."

"I appreciate that," Cedric said.

Roger got up and walked over to Cedric. "Do you

need anything before I go?"

Cedric smiled and shook his head.

"Then I'll see you around nine o'clock tomorrow morning."

"Thank you, my friend."

Roger left and Cap leaned back in the hospital chair.

"Just try to get some sleep," Cap said. "If you need anything, let me know."

Cedric nodded and closed his eyes. The truth is he remembered everything that had happened.

The hours dragged on like an insurance lecture. Several times during the night Cedric was awakened by severe pain and reached around his waist to find the magic button that would release pain meds into his system.

Finally the sun from the dawn filled the curtains. Cedric stared at the clock on the wall. It read 7:30. He knew what he had to do.

"Hey."

Cap snoozed away, snoring occasionally. Cap had been a fireman for Frenchtown since two years after graduating high school. He still had the exact same build except for his midsection was a tad thicker. Aside from that and a mustache, he looked almost exactly like he did when he was in high school.

"Hey!"

"Huh?" Cap said opening his eyes. "Are you okay?"

"Yeah, I'm fine," Cedric answered. "It's morning. Why don't you go to the cafeteria and get you something to eat? I know you must be hungry."

"No, I'm okay."

"Seriously?" Cedric asked. "You've known me this long and don't know why I'm asking?"

Cap laughed. He stood up and stretched. "Okay. What do you want me to sneak past the nurses' station?"

Cedric smiled. "A Diet Coke and a cup with ice."

"Really? That's all?"

"No, just one other tiny thing."

Cap smirked. "What?"

"I could really go for some scrambled eggs and a sausage biscuit, but not from the cafeteria here."

"From where then?"

Cedric smiled. "Hardees is just across the parking lot. I have some money in my pants, wherever they are."

Cap pointed to the cheap fake-wood wardrobe. "They're in there, but I'll get it for you."

"I owe you one."

Cap laughed. "One?" He put on his jacket and walked out the door.

There was a chill in the morning air as Cap walked the distance to the fast-food restaurant. He entered and got in line to order. He ordered the meal, which also came with hash rounds, and purchased the Diet Coke there as well.

He entered the hospital again and took the elevator back up to the second floor. When he walked back in the room the bed was empty. The metal stand that holds the meds and blood was also gone.

"Cedric, you're not supposed to get up." He could hear the water running in the shower of the bathroom. "You could have let the nurses give you a bath. That would have been much more fun." He placed the bag with the food on the bed table, which had rollers on the base to slide it up for the patients to eat, and took out the little container of hash rounds. He sat back in his chair and munched away.

A few minutes later, outside the front entrance, Madison dropped off Roger. "Call me if you need me to pick you up."

"Thanks, sweetie," he replied, "but I'm sure I can catch a ride with Cap." He went up to Cedric's room, entered, and looked confused. "Where is he?"

Cap nodded toward the bathroom. "Taking a shower."

"You weren't supposed to let him get up."

Cap shrugged. "He did it while I was gone to get him some breakfast."

Roger sat in the other chair, and they both waited. Before long they both had the same thought and walked over to the bathroom door and knocked. They called out but received no answer.

Roger rushed out to the nurses' station to get them to come unlock the bathroom door. They were not surprised when they found it empty.

"Let's go," Cap said grabbing his wallet from the end table.

He and Roger rushed out to the parking lot.

"Where's your car?" Roger asked.

"I thought it was right here." Cap looked around then he remembered leaving his keys by his wallet. He checked his pockets and stared at Roger. "Oh crap."

CHAPTER EIGHTEEN

Cedric opened the door and walked inside the building. He paused to clear the cobwebs and continued on down the aisle. He noticed the statues of saints high on the walls and the large organ pipes running up to the ceiling behind the stage. It was as foreign a place to him as anywhere he had ever been and he soaked in his surroundings. He made a beeline to the area he was searching for and stood there several seconds with his eyes closed.

"Cedric?"

"Oh, hello, Father." Cedric turned briefly to acknowledge the Catholic priest then continued with what he was doing. His hands shook as he placed a candle at the altar and used another candle to light it.

"I don't think I've seen you here lately," the priest said as he walked up beside him. "In fact, I'm not sure I've ever seen you in here."

Cedric looked all around the sanctuary of the church including to the ceiling. "No, sir, I guess I've never been in here before."

"That's okay. I'm glad you're here now. Did you come for confession?"

Cedric shook his head. "I'm afraid I don't have that much time and it might only frighten you."

The priest smiled and shook his head.

Cedric patted the priest on the shoulder. "But I will ask that you say a prayer for me tonight."

The priest was stunned. "Of course I will, my son. Please don't be offended, but I do every night."

Cedric nodded and turned to walk away.

"May I ask?" the priest asked.

Cedric stopped in the hallway, looking down the aisle and back.

"Who is the candle for?"

Cedric smiled. "For me, Father. It's for me."

Cedric drove from the church to the grocery store. He took a cart, more for balance than anything else since his cane was not in the hospital room when he left, and began to pick out several familiar items. He paid for it and took them out to Cap's car.

Then on he drove to his final destination. Cedric parked in the driveway, got out slowly, and took several bags of groceries out of the back seat. His knees hurt. Everything hurt. He felt faint and weak, an unfamiliar feeling for him to be sure, so he took each step carefully.

The sun was barely over the horizon and the grass still dripped with dew. Two cats darted off the porch as he approached the house.

He bent down gingerly, took the key from under the welcome mat, and let himself in the front door. Softly he strolled to the kitchen, opened the refrigerator door, and began taking the items out of the plastic bags and loading them onto the shelves. Then he walked through the double glass doors in the small dining room and into the backyard.

Roxy sat on a stool with her back to him as she guided the small paintbrush over the canvas. Small drips of oil paint decorated the ground in front of her feet. A large nylon bag with stripes the color of a rainbow sat beside the legs of the easel, a long handle draped over the edge of the bag. The painting of a mountainous landscape was about half complete.

Cedric walked up behind her and stared over her shoulder at the canvas. "May God have mercy on my soul should I ever see that painting completed."

Roxy smiled and turned around. "Painting is a journey, not a destination."

Cedric took his seat on the same concrete bench that used to sit in front of Roxy's home. "I'm beginning to believe this artistic undertaking of yours has no destination."

"You're early today," Roxy said.

"Yes. It's been a crazy day. An old friend is coming to visit today, one I have expected for some time, though not quite this early. I explained that I have a standing commitment on Saturdays, one I could not miss, not even for him. But I will have to greet him soon."

"Aw," Roxy said. "I was hoping you could stay all day."

"I would if I could, but unfortunately it's not up to me."

"Can you at least stay until lunch?"

Cedric nodded. "I will certainly try."

"Well then, tell me some news. What's happening at the newspaper and around town? Any thrilling stories to report?"

"Oh yes," Cedric said. "Thrilling indeed. Let's see where to begin. Saturday the 15th, the city voted to replace the stop sign at the high school with an actual traffic light."

Roxy nodded and continued to paint.

Cedric continued. "The Frosty Freeze has decided to join the 21st century and they have added salads and a tofu burger to their menu."

"That is exciting," Roxy said. "Have you tried the tofu burger?"

Cedric laughed but ignored the rhetorical question. "The Frenchtown Cavaliers finished the season with a 4-7 record. The elusive search for the third championship title continues. They think next year will be their year.

"Creative vandals inserted red dye into the nozzles at the do-it-yourself carwash. Roger's white Chrysler is now a beautiful shade of pink.

"Miss Hornsworth, our old English teacher, has finally retired from Frenchtown High after thirty-five years of faithful service.

"The Native American rain dance was scheduled for Wednesday at noon in the town park. However, it was cancelled on account of rain.

"Mr. Hunicutt, the town historian, hit a ten-point buck in his old Volkswagen Beetle on Route 6. He has asked the town council to relocate the deer-crossing sign so deer will stop crossing there."

Roxy giggled at that one.

"And," Cedric continued, "Saturday the 22nd —"

"Go on," Roxy said. But there was silence. She

looked around and saw Cedric slumped over and uncon-
scious. "Cedric!" she yelled, dropping the paintbrush on
the grass and rushing to him. "Cedric!"

Cedric opened his eyes.

"What's wrong?" Roxy asked. "What happened?"

"It's nothing," Cedric said, trying to regain his
composure. "My old football injuries revisit me on occa-
sion. It will pass in a moment." He sat upright and took
a deep breath. "There, it is gone."

Roxy sat beside Cedric and held his arm. "We all
have our old wounds, don't we? Mine lies in that bag."
She pointed to the striped bag on the ground. "It's in the
form of a letter, the only thing besides pictures I have.
It's faded and hard to read now, but it moves me still."

"Chris's letter?" Cedric asked. "Did you not say
that I could read it one day?"

Roxy was surprised and looked up into Cedric's
eyes. "You want to read it?"

"Yes. I want to read it. I would like to read it today
if you will let me."

Roxy slowly rose and sat back on her stool. Her
motions seemed uncertain as her trembling hand reached
down into the bag and pulled out an old envelope that
was once white but now layered with the yellow tint of
time. She handed it to Cedric. "Go ahead then. Read."

Cedric took the old envelope and looked at it for
several seconds. He pulled the multi-page letter from the
envelope, being careful not to damage the fragile petals
of the love letter. He opened it and looked at the first
page. He noticed the small water stains that he had tried
so hard to convince Chris were not from his tears. He

had lied of course. Emotions overpowered him and he held the letter close to his heart. Looking at Roxy, he wondered for a second if he should continue. He made his decision and began to read.

"Dear Roxy. Today I die. The boy I once knew is gone."

"Yes," Roxy said. "Please read it out loud."
Cedric continued.

"He is gone, my love, and it is because of you. I will miss him all the more. But the man has taken his place to stand beside you for all eternity. Only a man can love you the way I love you. Only a man has a heart large enough to hold the feelings that our love commands. From the moment you heard me tell you in my own voice what you meant to me, I have been under your spell. You have become my entire world."

Roxy looked straight ahead over her painting. "How you read it — his letter."

"Everything I see reflects the color in your cheeks. Everything I hear mimics your voice. Everything I smell belies your fragrant perfume."

"His letter," Roxy said. "You read it so well and yet so familiar."

```
    "Everything I touch feels like
your arms around me in the dark. Ev-
erything I taste has no flavor like
your kiss. It's as if my senses did
not exist before we met. Yet now ev-
erything I see, hear, smell, touch,
and taste is multiplied by your pas-
sion and ignites a fire in my heart. "
```

"There's something strange here," Roxy said. Cocking her head to the side and still looking over her painting, she seemed to be trying to focus harder on understanding this confusion.

Cedric continued without even looking at the paper.

```
    "I love how your bangs tickle
your eyebrows, how you have a way of
tilting your head when you find some-
thing amusing, how you roll your eyes
in protest."
```

"There's something going on I don't understand," Roxy said.

Cedric's vision took on a far-away stare as he recited his own words he had written so long ago.

"That voice. I know that voice." She turned to

see Cedric reciting the letter from memory. "A voice I remember hearing long ago outside my window."

> "No matter where I am, the wind brings thoughts of you. Your kiss is carried on the breeze and it softly caresses my lips."

Roxy got up, walked over and stood in front of him, and grabbed his hand.

Cedric suddenly realized she was there and quickly put the letter before his face again. "Uh, where was I?"

"And how can you read those faded words now?" Roxy asked. "You wrote it, didn't you?"

Cedric shook his head.

"The words were all you," Roxy said as she sat beside him and took his arm again. "It was all you, wasn't it?"

"No, Roxy."

"The letters were all you. The sweet words. The soul. It was all you."

"No."

"And the sweet voice outside my window in the darkness. It was you. It was always you, and I should have realized it every time I heard you call my name."

"I swear it wasn't," Cedric offered weakly. "I never loved you."

"Yes, you loved me," Roxy replied. "You love me still."

"No. No. No!" he offered louder.

"That was a mighty 'No,'" Roxy said. "In all these

twenty-eight years you've been the friend who brought me groceries and told me funny stories. Why did you not tell me? All those years ago, everything I loved came from you. You knew those were your tears on the paper. You knew that. You knew Chris gave me nothing."

Cedric handed the letter back to her. "He gave you his all. Even if it wasn't enough, he gave you everything, including his heart."

Suddenly the back door slid open and Cap and Roger came running into the backyard.

"There he is," Cap yelled. "I can't believe it. It's madness."

They rushed up to Cedric and Roxy on the bench.

"Oh no," Roger said. "It's suicide."

"What's going on?" Roxy asked.

"He's killed himself leaving the hospital this way," Roger answered.

"Cedric? What has happened?"

Cedric clearly didn't care for the interruption. "I did not finish telling you all the town gossip. Friday night behind the Frosty Freeze, Cedric Deburr was killed, murdered in cold blood."

"What have they done to you?" Roxy began to cry as she held Cedric's arm.

"They tricked me," Cedric said. "As intelligent as I always thought myself to be, it turns out I'm as gullible as they come. All my dreams of going out in glory in some grand arena fighting gods and giants have vanished. No, my battlefield was by the dumpster; my worthy adversary a Buick. It makes perfect sense. I have missed out on everything in my life. Now I have missed out on my own death."

Roxy jumped up and rushed toward the house. "I'll call 911."

"No. Please stay. I don't think I will make it until you return."

Roxy came back and knelt in front of Cedric, placing her head on his knee. "I love you."

Cedric stroked her hair. "That would make a wonderful fantasy, like *Beauty and the Beast*. But in the fairytale, when Beauty proclaimed her love, all his ugliness disappeared like magic. But you can see that I have not changed at all."

"I have done this to you. It's my fault," Roxy said.

"Don't be silly," Cedric said.

"Yes, it's all my fault."

"You are the reason for a lot of things," Cedric said, "but not this. You are the reason I got up every morning. My dad left when I was very young. My mom never wanted to be a single mom, at least not to a child like me. I never had a sister. As I got older I was always afraid girls would laugh at me, so I've never gotten close enough to find out. But because of you I have known a woman's heart and passion. I've had the gift of a friendship so true I could always wrap myself in it and stay protected by it."

Roxy cried harder. "I have only loved one man in my life, and now I will lose him for the second time."

"Do not cease to morn for Chris. He deserves no less. He was the best in all of us. I would ask only that whenever you visit his grave, that you drop one flower on mine before you leave."

Roxy cried uncontrollably. "Oh, my love."

Cedric started getting dizzy. "No, not like this. Not sitting down." He rose to his feet but stumbled.

Cap and Roger grabbed him by each arm.

Cedric pushed them away and took several unsteady steps forward. "I don't need your help." He turned to face his friends. "I never needed anyone. I'll face this alone."

Cedric turned around completely making a 360 degree circle as if searching for something, for someone. "I can feel him approaching. I feel his ice-cold breath. I hear his scythe dragging the ground. Well come on then. You will find me ready." Cedric raised his fist.

"No," Roxy said and rushed toward him, but Cap grabbed her.

"He's hallucinating," Cap said.

The three of them could do nothing but watch.

"I see him now, the Grim Reaper," Cedric said with a smile. "I see him. He's smiling. No, he's laughing. He's laughing at my belly. Come on then." Cedric punched in the air. "I know all my enemies now: lies, deceit, corruption, hatred, denial." He continued to punch. "What? Who's there? Oh it's you, ego. I knew you would catch me in the end. I will never stop. I'll fight to the end. We'll win the championship."

Cedric stumbled again but caught himself. Taking several deep breaths, he continued. "I have nothing left to give. My roads were paved with the best intentions." He raised his right hand and looked to the sky. "I tried my best to live my life with honesty and conviction. I trust I did some things right in this world. Hear my prayer, Lord. Let me gaze upon those golden streets. I pray you will open the gates for me. I hope they open wide enough."

Cap continued to hold onto Roxy. Along with Roger, they could only watch and cry.

Cedric put both hands over his heart. "There's only one thing left to say. One thing to say to you Roxy and for you to know I said it. I... Love..."

Cedric fell to the ground and was gone.

The End

www.ingramcontent.com/pod-product-compliance
Lightning Source LLC
Chambersburg PA
CBHW050036180626
46810CB00002B/742